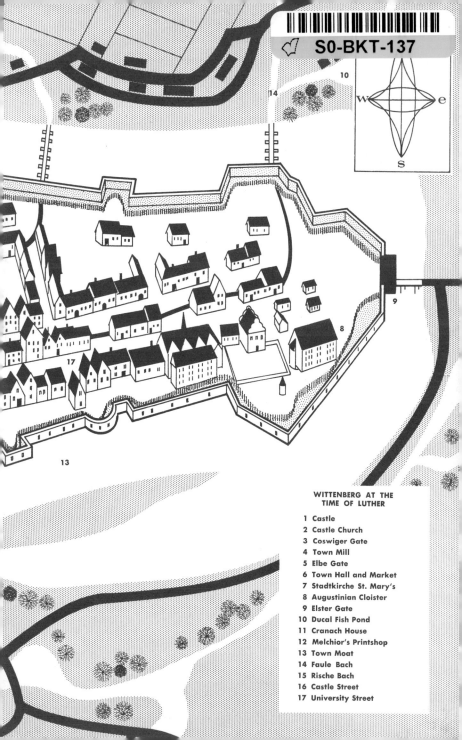

S0-BKT-137

**WITTENBERG AT THE
TIME OF LUTHER**

1 Castle
2 Castle Church
3 Coswiger Gate
4 Town Mill
5 Elbe Gate
6 Town Hall and Market
7 Stadtkirche St. Mary's
8 Augustinian Cloister
9 Elster Gate
10 Ducal Fish Pond
11 Cranach House
12 Melchior's Printshop
13 Town Moat
14 Faule Bach
15 Rische Bach
16 Castle Street
17 University Street

printer's
devil
from
wittenberg

THEODORE J. KLEINHANS

Illustrated by Vergal Buescher

AUGSBURG PUBLISHING HOUSE

Minneapolis, Minnesota

PRINTER'S DEVIL FROM WITTENBERG

CONTENTS

CHAPTER ONE

ADVENTURE
IN WITTENBERG

The clatter of hooves echoing across the meadow stopped seventeen-year-old Tilman von Rothenau in mid-stride. The boy saw two squires of about his own age faithfully practicing the art of jousting. They galloped headlong across the turf, in the full helmets and vizors of knighthood, but without body plates or horse armor. Their lances were blunt and padded, though the crashing of their arms nevertheless sounded as if a tourney were in full swing.

Fifty yards away Tilman halted. Half-shaded by a young beech he plopped his lanky frame onto a hillock of grass and loosened his pack. The pliant leather case hung limp, for it held only an extra shirt, bread and cheese, a prayer book, a letter from his mother, and

5

a loden jacket, which the mid-morning sun, in a sky marked only by high-flying dabs of cirrus cloud, long ago had caused Tilman to peel from his shoulders.

Tilman stretched out his lean legs and nibbled at a sliver of cheese. For three days now he had traveled through the dense firs of the Thuringian forest, and after the monotonous string of woodland villages and clearings he welcomed the sight of the fertile valley of the Elbe and the massive towers of Wittenberg.

He had spent the night at Kirchtraun, at a crossroads inn, and after three hours of hiking, despite a rather soggy breakfast of cold pork and oatmeal porridge, he was feeling a slight pang of hunger. For July the breezes of dawn had been sharp, but now with the sun halfway to its zenith and the larks skimming effortlessly above the river he could not have wanted a more tempting day.

Despite the fact that he was only seventeen, Tilman smiled condescendingly at the squires. More than others his age he could claim to be a man who knew what was going on in the world. In the year of our Lord 1520, he mused, didn't they realize the flower of knighthood had wilted? Didn't they know this was a brave new world where gunpowder could pierce the finest armor, where Spanish galleons were discovering a vast new continent in the Western Ocean? They might just as well be learning to make mud pies or spin a top. Knighthood was dead.

He finished his snack of cheese and brown bread and examined the city that spread out on the far bank of the Elbe. Proudest of all were the turreted walls and the sturdy drawbridges, spanning a moat at least the width of the jousting ground. Between the river and the moat he could make out the earthen breastworks and a trellised walkway, roofed over to keep off the rain and snow.

Far off to the left he saw the elector's castle, with the spire of the Schlosskirche marking the western edge of town. Directly before him rose the gable of the city hall, and not far to the right the sturdy walls of the Augustinian cloister.

As a native Saxon he had heard much of Wittenberg. It was not a proud city, in the sense of Worms or Mainz or Frankfurt, but it did serve as the home of Duke Fredrick, at least for part of the year, and its young university was already gaining fame. Given time, it might outgrow Tilman's home town of Torgau.

Tilman had only one reason for stopping at Wittenberg: the Castle Church. For years he had been hearing of its splendor, and even though it was a few miles off the route to Mainz, he owed it a visit. In the bright haze he could make out the Gothic splendor of the spire, pointing high toward its Maker, and as he studied it he yearned for a closer look.

The church itself was the utmost the duke could

make it—a showpiece of marble and mosaic and frescoes and canvas. It had seen the loving care of masters like Dürer and Cranach and Mabuse and Barbari, the best artists Italy and the Netherlands and Germany could offer. What made it a meeting ground for pilgrims was its storehouse of relics, a collection that far outstripped Frankfurt and Cologne and could hardly have been far behind the glories of St. John Lateran or St. Paul's Outside the Gates in Rome.

At the Latin school in Torgau Tilman had heard it described so lovingly and in such fine detail by the Brothers of the Common Life that he felt he already knew it by heart, with its three marble galleries built high up above the porticoes of the nave, the glitter of gold and silver showcases, the bits and pieces from the lives of Christ and Mary and the Apostles.

Above the castle Tilman noted the quartered flag emblazoned with the ducal coat-of-arms, a sure sign Fredrick was now in Wittenberg. The whole town, in fact, fluttered with pennons and streamers, even the bridges across the Elbe.

Odd, thought Tilman, unless it was an annual market day or a local festival. In that case, the Castle Church might be so crowded with tourists he would be forced to spend the night, and finish his sightseeing on the morrow.

A few cottages, usually built of wattle and mud with

a simple thatched roof, poked above the bottomlands. The river flowed sleepily beneath the bridge, and although there was only a pair of fishermen casting their nets into the waters, dozens of empty skiffs on the banks showed that fishing was an occupation as well as a sport.

A little parade of ducks waddled toward the hillock where Tilman sat musing, first the mother and then the brood of ducklings. She picked at the crumbs from his mid-morning snack, gobbled them down, and scolded him for not leaving enough for the young ones.

Tilman rose slowly and sauntered across the bridge. So far his trip had been pleasant. In another two weeks he would be in Mainz. And whether or not he stopped to put it in words, his heart told him that life was good.

At Torgau he had left no one. His father, long ago knighted as a *Freiherr* and awarded with a country estate, had died in battle for the same prince who once conferred the title. Tilman was two then. For the growing boy his mother had been both father and mother.

When he was ten she entrusted his schooling to the Common Life Brothers, from whom he had drunk deep of the learning of his day. Now his mother was gone too, a victim of the plague. Once his guardians had paid off the loans on the estate, Tilman could no longer reckon himself a son of wealth.

To be honest, he did have fifteen gulden secreted

about his person—sewn into the hem of his jacket, hidden beneath the flap of his pack, and tucked into a secret fold of his belt. In Torgau he had deposited another forty, for which he bore a letter of credit. The letter he considered precious, to be used only to set up a printing press, or to buy a house when he married, or for some urgent need.

He was a bit pleased to know he was not penniless, even if the plain stuff of his jacket and trousers and boots would have denied he once came of rich parents. What money he could call his own was scarcely more than a master blacksmith could earn in a good year— not a fortune, but a nice nest egg. What Tilman considered even more valuable was the fine education he had stored away and the skills he had learned on the presses of the brothers.

Now he was off to Mainz, largely at their suggestion. He already knew the art of composing type, mixing ink, justifying lines, locking up a chase, planning the gatherings. Of all places in Germany, the monkish printers had advised him, Mainz was the capital of the printing trade. With the exception of Venice and perhaps Paris, he could learn more in Mainz than anywhere.

In his pack he carried a Latin prayer book. Both because it was the last gift from his mother, for his seventeenth birthday, and because it was so fine a product of the printer's art, he valued it even more highly than his letter of credit. It had come from the presses of Aldus in Venice, with overprinting in two colors, and the platework and woodcuts and typeface and registry and paper and binding were a noble tribute to the skills of the bookmaker.

Unlike his father, who had won his titular spurs as a knight in battle, Tilman loved books. He was not sure if his love for printing came from his pursuit of learning, or vice versa, but he did know the printing press had suddenly opened a broad new frontier, and that for the moment it could work far more good than those new continents Columbus had been discovering.

He had learned just enough from the printers of the Latin school to know how exciting the printing trade could be. At the book fairs or sometimes in the abbot's library he had been allowed to handle the best and newest products of the press. By now learning the art of printing, like the glow of first love, seemed the noblest goal this side of paradise.

His father had cousins in Mainz who were grocers, and of course they might prove helpful, providing a roof over his head if his gulden melted too quickly away. With luck, he might not only attach himself to a master printer but even buy a small share in a press, if he managed to hold onto the forty gulden in his letter of credit. At the very least he would learn the trade from the best artisans in all Germany, and that in itself was a worthwhile goal.

He left the fertile gardens and orchards stretching between the river and the moat and approached the drawbridge. The planking was worn and splintered from the iron rims of decades of wagons, and he trod with care not to catch his boot in the cracks.

From the open balustrade of the watchtower a pair of guards examined him leisurely. He appeared to be a country lad come to market, perhaps an apprentice or student, totally unarmed and peaceable. They allowed him to pass unchallenged, with scarcely a second glance.

Once inside, he was quite disappointed. The streets were narrow and dusty, even those that were crudely paved. Pigs and chickens darting before his path made it seem more like a country village than a walled town with a ducal palace.

Occasionally a fine three-story house of brick or stone, with bull's-eye windows and a roofed entryway, proudly fronted the street, but most of the dwellings were hardly more than cottages, with roofs of thatch or tile, and with garbage and fodder thrown helter-skelter into the street.

Despite its poverty and uncouthness, the town wore an air of excitement. The urchins who dashed tirelessly about, although their clothing was frayed and dirty, acted as if they were enjoying a holiday. Even a block from the market place Tilman could hear the excited buzz of the crowd. It seemed to hover in the air, almost like the proud gables of the city hall or the twin towers of St. Mary's just behind. He turned the corner of the Eibgasse and found himself in a crowd of holiday-makers swarming in on the square from every point of the compass.

A tiny stream scarcely five steps wide ran leisurely along the length of the square. A wall of paving stones kept the stream to a narrow channel. Half-a-dozen catwalks crossed it, and beneath the tapered sycamores on the far bank the stalls of the vendors backed up against the stream.

Tilman's ears rang with the noise of the shoppers' chatter and the cries of the vendors, but after his three-day tramp through the stillness of the firs, with only the call of the cuckoo, he could do with a taste of civilization again. Wittenberg was not really so different from Torgau, he mused. Despite the plain cottages and the garbage, doubtless there were many who were proud to call it home.

The flow of traffic seemed to center on the town hall, where a rough platform had been built. A dozen men bustled about on the wooden framework, dressed in the satins and broadcloths of the well-to-do. Two wore golden chains of office proclaiming their position on the town council. They sat leisurely near the gallows, chatting happily.

At first glimpse Tilman thought there was to be a hanging, but as he examined the peculiar boxes on the platform he decided they were cages, not for human prisoners but for animals. This was not just a market day, it was a public hunt. And a hunt in which all the townsmen and country folk could share, not just the duke and a few to whom he had granted hunting rights, was not an everyday occurrence. It was no wonder the square was swarming with humanity: with peasants, still with the smell of earth and cattle about them; with students, rather wild-looking with their knives and clubs, even though they did wear somber black capes as a sign of their profession; with townsfolk, fishermen, maid servants, millwrights, traders, shop-keepers, tailors, monks, waggoners, shoemakers, fish-wives.

The market was such a hubbub Tilman quietly crossed a catwalk and paused for a minute beside the line of stalls. Before him the people seethed like a school of herring. He wondered how they could move at all. The sunlight filtered through the leaves of the plane trees and cast a checkered shadow on Tilman's face. An unruly mop of blond hair stuck out over his fore-head.

He admired the finely-bedecked wives of the burghers, with baskets on their arms and purses in hand, often with a housemaid and perhaps a troupe of three or four children in tow. He wondered at the endless flow of students and what seemed to be an equal number of monks.

The market had a varied aroma and garb. There was a heavy scent of fish and the earthy taint of beets and turnips. The green of the cabbages contrasted with the orange of the carrots. Above the clamor Tilman occasionally could make out the crowing of a cock, soundly trussed up in a wooden cage, or the bleat of a lamb or kid.

Across the way Tilman's eye fell by chance on a charming country girl who was busy heaping up a stack of cabbages that a band of unruly boys had knocked over. In a yellow dirndl and a fawn-colored smock she looked fresh and neat, just coming into the full bloom of womanhood. She moved with the grace of a deer, effortlessly, and her cheeks bore the bright blush of a girl who spends her life in the sun. Her hair was dark, almost to the point of being raven, which was striking in one whose skin was so fair. Even at twenty feet Tilman could see that her dirndl had been patched often and that the skirt had been let out, though for a girl who had wheeled a barrow of vegetables and cheese over a dusty road from some outlying village she appeared remarkably fresh and clean.

The stall was hardly five feet wide, and the girl's wares were spread out on the shelving furnished by the town. The turnips she displayed bore the fresh mauve color of the first of the season, about the size of young beets. She also had a range of leafy vegetables such as spinach, kale, shepherd's purse, leek and radishes, and, for good measure, a pile of carrots. Her real stock in trade, however, appeared to be cheese. There were small round balls of it hung in fine netting, rolls cut into small cartwheels, soft cheeses with a moldy blue crust already beginning to scent the stall.

When Tilman looked at her closely he thought he could detect goat hairs caught in the fabric of her dirndl. The picture he envisioned was that of a country shepherdess from one of the nearby villages, come to market to sell the family wares.

Six or eight youngsters swept across the passageway and diverted his attention. They were playing on the rough pavement with clay marbles, and in their excitement they were pushing and crowding and crawling under the feet of the older and the more sedate. One salty tradesman cursed them, but like most youngsters they did not even look up from their game.

Starting at the platform, a great shout rolled across the square, working its way out to the edges of the crowd and then echoing from the houses and shops back to the market place. With a clanging of gates and a shrieking of voices the caged game sprang for freedom. The hunt was on!

As the wooden boxes swung open Tilman could see the game—a pair of young stags, a wild boar, crates of rabbits and hares, and several cages of grouse. The birds' feathers had been clipped, and they were stuffed to the gizzards with corn to keep them from flying too high, although they still could soar up to twenty or thirty feet.

The rabbits bolted through the forest of legs with a kind of desperation that added to the excitement. The boar had been partially detusked, with the sharpest of his razor-like weapons sawed away, but with the stubs and his two hundred pounds of bone and muscle, he was still a formidable fighter.

Almost at once the square became a battlefield. Knives, clubs, swords, nets, and sticks appeared as if by magic. Even the youngsters, the monks, and the *hausfraus* could not resist the temptation. Though they knew better than to tackle a boar or a stag, they at least could try for a hare or a grouse. With the rabbits dashing between one's legs and the grouse bouncing crazily off heads and shoulders, confusion reigned.

As a stranger Tilman was at the same time amused and resentful. In such close quarters how could so many people possibly swing clubs and knives without smashing into human flesh? He did not see any cross-bows or halberds or long bows, but even with less lethal weapons the sport appeared too risky.

A stag suddenly bounded high off the back of the platform and crashed headlong into a wall of the town hall, splintering an antler. From that moment the animal seemed crazed. He struck the wall again, blindly, and then in a mad dash skirted the edge of the square.

Perhaps the sight of the trees appeared like the safety of a forest, for he made straight for the brook, pursued by a howling mob of students. Egged on by the smell of the creek and a chance to escape he leaped high, as if to clear the line of stalls, but his hoof caught in the wooden framework. He spun and rolled into the midst of the youngsters playing marbles, just missing the girl who sold cheese.

Blind with fear and with the blood from his bruised skull, he lashed out with hooves and horns against the children. Almost as soon as the stag hit the pavement and skidded into the circle, Tilman Von Rothenau tensed. He drew the small cooking knife at his belt, but there was no time to get it open. He dove into the melee.

Dimly he felt a flash of pain as his knee crashed against the bricks and his hands caught at a horn. With his right hand he managed to grab the broken stub,

He managed to grab the broken stub.

sharp as it was, and while his left sought for the other, he was whipped violently over the stag's haunches.

Without really being aware of anything around him, even the screams of the children, he realized he had to hang on. He twisted and forced the taut muscles of the deer's neck as if he were holding the lever of a gigantic printing press. The beast writhed and squirmed, dashing the boy against the cobblestones. He could scarcely hear the cries of the crowd. Perhaps because of his patrician training, which said a squire must look first after his people, he was aware only that he must protect the youngsters.

The hooves thrashed past Tilman's face and thudded into his groin. He winced with pain. Blood oozed into his palms and his grip on the horns loosened. As if in a dream he noted a dozen hands pushing against the stag holding it captive. Lying quietly, seeing only the blue sky overhead, his head reeled. He tried to stretch out, but the pain in his side was too intense. He fell unconscious.

CHAPTER TWO

A DOMINICAN CALLER

The afternoon sun streamed in through the windows, which were flung open to the air, and danced over the linen coverlet. Tilman von Rothenau lay propped against the headboard. His face was pale but a wan smile played over his cheeks. Beyond the leaded glass lay the city of Wittenberg.

Two blocks away, at the corner of the town wall, rose the turrets of the castle and the spire of the church, a hazy yellow in the warm glint of the sun. For two weeks now he had been an unwilling guest in Wittenberg. He still had not seen the silver showcases and the golden reliquaries of the Schlosskirche that had attracted him in the first place.

In the hall and on the steps he heard the sound of shuffling feet. Little Hans Cranach hobbled through the door on a crutch, with his leg in splints, hopping along like a toy soldier with a wooden leg.

"Hello, Hansel."

"Hello, Tilman. Feeling better today?"

"Yes, thank you. The chicken broth and the dumplings tasted good, and in a few days I'd like to have a real look at your town."

"Can I go along?"

A square-shouldered burgher, taller than most and with an air of kindly authority, came through the door behind Hans. He must have been nearly fifty, to judge from the close-cropped hair and the neatly trimmed beard, cut short and with a double point like a W. There appeared a certain strength of character in the flaring nostrils, the heavy brows, and the ears tight against the head.

"*Guten Tag,* Tilman," said the older Cranach. "*Wie geht's denn heut?*"

"Fine, Master Lucas, thanks to all the care you've given me. This is the first day I've really wanted out of bed."

"That's a good sign. Dr. Pergesius will be pleased. He hasn't been here today, has he?"

"No. This week he comes every second day. Hansel looks as if he's recovered, too."

"A broken leg is the least of it. Every boy can expect one of those. But you! For a while we thought we would lose you. Out of your head with fever, twisting in pain, and calling for your mother and Saint Elizabeth. But thank the good Lord, all that is past. And faithful old Pergesius deserves some of the credit too."

"The pain is almost gone. Now that the stitches are out, perhaps I can travel in a week or two."

"No more'n a fish could fly! The doctor says you'll stay put for a month. I guessed you might feel that way so I asked him. Even with the wound healing, he says you're to take life easy. A punctured intestine can be sewed together, but you need time to get your strength back. None of this twenty-miles-a-day business, or eating salt pork at a country inn, or running from highwaymen."

"But what will I do? I can't pay board forever and a doctor's bill too."

"There'll be no board to pay, and no doctor's bill. You don't think Frau Barbara and I would move from our own bedroom and give it to you, do you, if we thought of you as a paying guest? Our firstborn might be dead, if it weren't for your bravery, and this is the least we can do. Besides, with the mob of apprentices in the studios and the housemaids to run the place, one more or less makes no difference. I know what you'll say. Who wants to spend his youth in the studios of a minor court painter in an out-of-the-way watering spot in Thuringia? I have the answer to that too. Since you won't be able to travel for five or six weeks, perhaps you'd like to see something of Barbara's brother, Melchior Klein. He's a printer—one of Wittenberg's best. There are scores of them here, with all the writing the professors turn out, and I think he can teach you something. You may not be able to do much, with a cramp in your belly, but at least it'll make you feel you're not wasting your time."

Tilman really had not thought very far into the future. For ten days he had hovered on the brink of life and death, while Dr. Pergesius tended him almost hourly with purges of horehound and beef broth and mustard plasters and bloodletting and belladonna. His thoughts had been so occupied with pain, in his half-conscious state, that there had been little time for anything else.

"Will I be able to travel before snowfall?"

"Easily. If not, we'll send you along to Mainz by stage. This is scarcely August and you'll be fit as a horse by October."

In the days he had been a patient Tilman had come to know and like Lucas Cranach. Cranach was the court painter, a town councilman, the town druggist, the owner of the biggest house in Wittenberg and several others besides, and no minor figure.

Across the courtyard in the far wing lay the master artist's studios, where more than a score of helpers, ranging from apprentices in their teens to master artists in their fifties, toiled through the hours of daylight with brushes and pens. Commissions flooded in not merely from the court but also from nobles and burghers throughout northern Europe who desired a canvas with the coveted signature of Lucas Cranach.

Standing in Tilman's room in the glow of the afternoon sun, the artist appeared more a businessman than a painter. With the vast painting factory he ran, where he did scarcely more than the initial sketch and the final touch-up, in a sense he *was* a businessman.

"Tilman, there's one thing about the affair that will please you. The hunt, I mean."

"What's that, Master Lucas?"

"The council has voted to ban it. It's always been dangerous, with a sprinkling of bashed knees and fingers, though, of course, nothing ever quite as bad as the crazed stag. We've been having the chases for a hundred years now, as a royal favor from the duke, and they've become traditional. But there'll never be another one. At least not with boars and stags."

"Not even with rabbits, Daddy?" pleaded little Hans.

"Well, maybe. We'll have to see. Of course, the ordinary folk can't hunt wild game at all, and this is their one chance. But with half the crowd drunk and the animals wild, the risk is simply too great. We conferred with the duke's secretary, and His Grace agreed the hunts should be banned. By the way, he also sent formal greetings and a wish for your speedy recovery."

"Duke Fredrick?"

"The same. He heard of your gallantry from Spalatin, his secretary. If the stag hadn't been stopped, it might have killed a dozen youngsters."

Cranach peered from the bull's-eye windows down over the courtyard. The house was a huge L-shaped one with three stories and a garret. The painter also owned the two smaller buildings which completed the four sides of the square. In the near wing the ground floor was a part of the studios and the classrooms. The second floor served as quarters for Lucas's family, and the third and fourth sheltered relatives and servants.

In the far wing the students and apprentices occupied the upper stories, shut off from the family and the maids but still under the watchful eye of the master. Because Cranach had always been such a close acquaintance of the elector and a friend of the university, he sometimes turned over the garret to half-a-dozen scholars, not necessarily those who were interested in painting, but budding lawyers or doctors or teachers.

As Cranach watched he heard from the gate the clangor of the bell. A house girl answered and Cranach saw the gaunt frame of Frater Heidrich. Wearing a dirty black robe, the Dominican monk bowed low, made the sign of the cross, and entered. The girl bowed in return, and crossed her breast.

"You have company, Tilman," said Cranach. "Frater Heidrich. Do you remember him?"

"No, not really. I vaguely remember there was a priest here, giving the viaticum. But who he was or what he said, I couldn't say."

"That shows how serious your condition was. He wasn't here at all, but at the market. I'll say this for him, though I do think the Dominicans are far too cunning. He *was* Johnny-on-the-spot, thought you were on the verge of death, and promptly dug out his holy oils and rosary to get you to purgatory."

"I wish he'd have come back sooner. I could have used him those days when I hung between heaven and hell."

"He probably figured you were dead. Anyway, his job was done. Locked away in that monastery, they don't know what's happening. Besides, burying's the job of the Augustinians, not the Dominicans. They're the preachers at the Stadtkirche. The town parish, I mean."

The monk's sandals clopped across the cobblestones. "He'll doubtless want to see you alone. Besides, he's a shade too unctuous for my taste. I prefer the Augustinians, who are more like ordinary people. I'll slip

across to the kitchen." He smiled as if he had pulled off
the diplomatic coup of the century. Tilman snickered.
Cranach was rich enough to hire a hundred priests, and
yet he was afraid of them.

The patient pushed the yellow hair back off his fore-
head. In the hall he could hear the slippers of the
maid and the sandals of the monk approaching. In a
moment the tall, spare figure of Brother Heidrich stood
beside the bed.

"Hello, Tilman. They tell me that's your name?"

"Yes, father. Thank you for giving me the last rites."

The priest self-consciously jerked his head, as if he
would do the same for any poor soul. "I really didn't
expect to see you alive. You were a sorry mess when I
last saw you." On so bright an afternoon the all-weather
cowl of the Dominican looked warm and out of place.

His face had a shadow of gloom, indicating that he
led the life of a hermit and ascetic.

"How was it you happened to be so near?"

"I was watching the hunt, like everyone else. I was
on my way to Kronberg, where I say mass. And of
course I always keep a vial of the oils about me." His
words were friendly, but his face had a far-away look.
He moved toward the window.

Toward the west and the north one could discern
the circle of the walls, with its turrets and watchtowers.

From Tilman's window on the second story the waters of the moat lay hidden behind the walls, but in the far distance the sunlight danced on the waters of the Elbe.

"I'd meant to read to you from St. Jerome, or perhaps a psalm. Maybe you'll also want to have a mass said, for you or your parents. It's only a few groschen, and you would feel a great load off your shoulders."

Tilman scooted higher on the pillow and acted as if he had not heard. He was a pious son of the church and had attended mass not only on Sundays and feast days but nearly every day of his life. There was a kind of slick insincerity about Frater Heidrich that he did not like.

"Ah, young man, but I see you have your own prayer book. That should be worth at least four or five masses." The Dominican reached across the pallet and picked up the prayer book. Bound in bleached pigskin and stamped with gold, the little octavo was indeed a work of art. As anyone who had ever held a book in his hand well knew, it was worth far more than the price of a few masses.

Tilman frowned. He did not like people handling the book at all, unless they had first asked permission. The woodprints were such a delight, and the folio capitals were so carefully painted with purple and silver, that he did not like the volume needlessly handled. In the rough hands of Frater Heidrich such a fine edition seemed totally out of place.

"That's my most precious possession. I do trust you'll handle it carefully."

The monk flushed. He took it nearer the light. "This is far too fine a book for a wandering apprentice. It ought to be in a library, such as ours." The monk's eyes gleamed almost frighteningly, and Tilman reddened with anger.

"No!"

"As I said, I'll say a few masses for your parents, if you'll give me their names. Besides, a monk knows far more Latin than you, and can make much better use of the book."

"I told you, no!"

"What you say doesn't really matter. It was I who gave you the viaticum and the last rites when you were delirious. Have you no gratitude for the gift of paradise?"

Tilman knotted his fist. He had never seen anyone quite so audacious and he did not know whether he ought to shout and create a scene or reason with the man.

"I tell you, that book was a gift from my sainted mother. It is an Aldine from Venice, which a man of your intelligence knows is worth the price of four cows, not four masses. I treasure it as my fondest keep-sake. I would not sell it for any price, and if you take it without my consent I shall report the theft to the council."

The monk did not bat an eye. "Who would believe a penniless student? Doubtless you stole it from a banker or a stall at the fair. Who would believe *your* word against that of Frater Heidrich, once my name is inscribed across the frontispiece?"

Tilman recalled that he had not signed his name, because the fine linen paper and the imprints were so perfect in every respect that he hated to blur them with his own name. For what comfort it was, he remembered that the family crest of the von Rothenaus was burn-ished into the back. Even so, the priest might mar it.

The boy could hardly contain himself. As weak as he was and although still confined to bed, he made a noble try. He sighed, almost like a mother with a disobedient child. "I've told you the book is mine. I do not wish to part with it, sell it, or even have others touch it, unless I have invited them. What more can I say?"

By now the monk was livid. What had appeared an easy conquest over a sickly apprentice was going against him. He breathed hard, between set teeth. "The book is mine. Don't you know the Scripture: 'The laborer is worthy of his hire'? Do you mean to deny a servant of God? The fires of hell plague you!" He took two angry strides toward the door. "If you do not try to cause trouble, I'll see that you get another prayer book, one more suited to your station in life."

From his bed the patient made an effort to get to his feet. The pain in his groin made him shudder. He had only one recourse, and that was to shout for help. He opened his mouth but the sound did not come out.

The huge figure of Lucas Cranach barred the door, and his chest almost touched that of the monk. Heidrich took a step back, in surprise. His face was puffy with anger.

"For shame, monk, that a man of God would steal from a sick boy."

Heidrich did not even seem to hear. "A curse on your whole house, and may all your children be bastards." His voice was so high-pitched it must have been heard throughout the courtyard. He slammed the book hard on the table and pushed the artist aside. Lucas let him pass. He fairly flew down the steps and through the door.

"I'll see you all rot in hell, and on earth too, just you see!" With a shake of the fist his flying robes disappeared on the far side of the wall.

CHAPTER THREE

PRINTER'S DEVIL

Lucas Cranach jerked at the bell rope and heard the insistent tinkle on the other side of the gate. A jumble of ivy spilled over the gateway, accented here and there with the scarlet of ramblers. To judge by the flowers the home might have been a country villa, not a tradesman's house on the Scharrengasse. But just behind the house rose the step-like gables of the town hall.

An apprentice, one of many "devils" in his brother's print shop, flung open the gate. His hands were stained black and his leather apron smelled of linseed and ink. He bowed slightly, with hips and knees, as an apprentice should when he recognized a master. "Good morning, Meister Lucas. Come in. Meister Melchior is in the composing room. I'll tell him you've come."

The courtyard could hardly have been twenty feet square, and the rough-hewn sandstone walls of the three-story house abutted a more recent two-story addition of half-timbered mortar. The double doors at the far end were thrown wide to the August air.

Lucas pulled at his dark green doublet and without vanity realized how striking it looked against the olive green of his trousers. Around his neck he wore the thin gold seal of a councilman, not solely because he had just come from the city hall and a meeting with the registrar, but because he wanted to make an especially good impression on his brother-in-law. Obviously he came with a request.

Before he had reached the printing shop his wife's sister, Lotte, leaned out through an upper window. Over her head she waved the goose wing with which she had been dusting. She was scarcely the most graceful person in the world, with her short and dumpy frame, and she looked almost like a fat goose trying to get off the ground. Lucas suppressed a laugh, though he could not check the grin.

"What a pleasant surprise, Lucas! We haven't seen you for weeks. Ever since little Hansel broke his leg. Did you want Melchior?" She was a pleasant soul, for all her chatter. Even if she seldom bothered to scour the pots or sweep out the hearth, she meant the best in the world.

"I could chat with you both, if you're not busy."

"Melchior is hard at work on a rush order, but he needs a break. Bring him along up. I made some cakes this morning, and we'll have blueberry spread and a pot of mint tea."

There was something about the printing shop that Lucas loved. He could never tell quite what it was. It may have been the distinct and exotic smells of linseed, ink, paper, leather, or drying agents like turpentine and shellac.

In the shed behind the huge screw press Lucas saw rack after rack of pages, drying and waiting to be folded, cut, collated, and bound. The racks beside the press filled quickly as a journeyman and an apprentice spelled each other rolling the ink and throwing the lever. Braced firmly against the floor and the roof with huge timbers, the press resembled the works of a man-of-war or perhaps the kind of levered catapult the Romans once used to besiege a fortress.

Piled high against the wall was a stack of chases ten high, locked up with type for the press. On the plaster wall a score of the more attractive placards and woodcuts that had come from the press were tacked haphazardly.

A little apart from the rest of the shop, where

leaded windows and a skylight allowed full use of the daylight, Melchior and a journeyman put type into their composing sticks with swift fingers. The font of type lay between them and their hands moved constantly back and forth, setting up the lines.

Lucas watched quietly. Only after two or three minutes did Melchior look up, and then with a touch of annoyance, as if he expected to hear an apprentice tell him that a frisket had cracked or a lockpin had broken, or that some other calamity demanded the master's skilled hand.

"Ah, Lucas, it's you. We haven't seen you for weeks. But then we've been rather busy."

"I see. Lotte just leaned from the window and said the water was boiling for tea. Sound appetizing?"

"Ordinarily, yes. Days like this she sometimes brings it right to the desk, so we don't lose time. But if we talk here we'll disturb Herman. Maybe I'll just join you. Mind you, only fifteen minutes."

"Good. Melchior, you work too hard. You know what Dr. Pergesius would say."

"Too hard?" The master printer rose to his feet, wiped his fingers on the apron, and smoothed back his hair. "Nobody ever worked too hard. What are *you* doing—out walking in the sun?"

Lucas laughed. "Partly. I've just signed a contract at the town hall, with the comptroller's seal. Besides, don't try to change the subject. You *do* work too hard. You've had your shop only two years, with half-a-dozen presses established far longer than yours. And already you're the biggest printer in Wittenberg."

"That's what comes of hard work, Lucas."

"So you earn your money twice as fast. But you also work twice as long, and will doubtless die twice as soon."

"Nobody ever died of too much work."

"That's not what Pergesius told you."

"At any rate my girls will own a house or two and a few acres of land."

"But with their father dead."

"Ah, now. Let's not argue, good brother-in-law. Besides, this time I have an excuse: the new type face I got last month from Paris. The elector saw a pamphlet we'd done two weeks ago, and he's requested the whole *Address to the German Nobility*. It's the one where Brother Martin flays Rome right down to the bone—the greed of the priests, the pope's crown, the priests' immorality, the crowning of human logic. The duke wants thirty copies in calf, to be sent out by the court, and a special one in tooled goatskin as a gift to his brother. Lufft has already sold out his edition, and we should have no trouble disposing of another 5,000."

"Aha, you'll be getting rich fast, Melchior." By now the two men had entered the doorway and were climb-

ing the steps to the living quarters. Lucas had struck a
tender spot.

"Not nearly so fast as the court painter. What with
thirty-odd assistants doing the work, and you getting
the pay. Even if you didn't make a pfennig off painting you could still live comfortably off the drugstore.
How many clerks do you have now, three? My wife
says the price of saltpeter has just jumped a groschen
a pound."

For all his good qualities Melchior still was sensitive
about his poverty-stricken youth on a rock-strewn farm,
and now that he had tasted money and had put his
vast energy to work he could think of little but success.

Lotte stood waiting at the head of the stairs and beck-
oned the menfolk into the sitting room. A housemaid
was laying out the last of the cups and cakes and pouring out the steaming mint.

"How's Hans?" asked Lotte.

"Fine, thank you. If Barbara weren't so watchful
he'd have thrown that crutch away a week ago. But
Pergesius says to keep him on it another few days, to
let the bone grow solid."

"How about the apprentice? Is he doing well too?"

"Tilman. Tilman von Rothenau. A young Freiherr's
son from Torgau. He's been out of bed for three days
now, and well beyond all danger. In fact, it's he I've
come to talk about."

A shadow crossed Melchior's face. "To us?"

"Yes. You see, Tilman wants to be a printer. Not here, but in Mainz. He'll not be able to travel for at least six weeks. Ten would be safer. Since you have one of the best print shops in Wittenberg and since he's dying to learn, I thought he might help you."

Lotte smiled. Melchior frowned, thinking perhaps of a clumsy country bumpkin upsetting the fonts and smearing ink all over the platens.

"He's spent a year with the Brothers of the Common Life at their shop in Torgau. He can talk intelligently about tympans and chases and compositor's sticks, and I think you'll find him no greenhorn. Frankly, I don't know. He has the most glorious edition of an Aldine I've ever laid eyes on. Matches anything in the castle."

Melchior still stood silent, but the prospect seemed to appeal to his wife. Their daughters had grown and married, and except for the maid and two apprentices the house stood quiet and empty. "You could use help, Melchior. Even if it's only to pull the sheets from the press and hang them on the drying rack. Lately, you've been working twelve hours a day, and I fear you'll be a case for the doctor."

"Mind you," Lucas went on, "he still couldn't run the press. The stitches have been out of his belly for only two days and he couldn't do any heavy lifting or pushing. Still, I think he'd be useful, and, just as important, I think he'd enjoy it and learn something."

Melchior's face still did not appear happy. Lotte tried to sway the argument. "We do have plenty of room, Melchior, and it wouldn't be so lonely with an extra mouth at the table. At night, when the journeymen go home, it would be pleasant to have company."

Lucas realized that his councilman's golden chain and the rich-looking green doublet were having little effect on the hard-headed printer. Melchior had deadlines to meet and money to bank, but perhaps not so warm a heart as Lucas for those who needed help.

"Lucas, just what did you have in mind?" The printer swallowed the last of his tea, as if eager to hurry back to the composing room.

"Try him for a week. At the latest he'll want to leave before snowfall. For his keep I'll be happy to pay five groschen a week. In my opinion he's skilled enough to deserve a wage, say ten groschen a week. I'll be happy to pay that too."

Melchior Klein's features softened noticeably, and after a minute's thought, broke into an open smile. "That's more than I pay a senior apprentice, Lucas."

"The others needn't know. Tilman is a youth of discretion, and for all they know, he can be a journeyman. Just treat him kindly and let him learn and do. If you prefer, I could continue to board him. It's only a five-minute walk. Still, he'll feel more a part of the shop if he lives with the others."

By now Melchior was all smiles. He was still eager to get back to work, but he knew well that he could make a profit on the board and room. With someone else paying the wages, the lad's work would cost nothing. Even if he could only run errands or sweep the floor, he would be worth something.

"All right," he said. "When would you like to send him?"

"In a day or two, I think. First I must ask Pergesius, and talk it over with Tilman. Don't work him too hard, and I hope you'll remember what he did for Hansel."

"We will, Lucas," said Lotte. "He won't be just an apprentice. He'll be one of the family."

"Good. I'll send word with a housemaid as soon as we can fix a date."

Melchior bounced happily down the hall, while Lucas and Lotte lingered over a second cup of tea.

CHAPTER FOUR

SIGNPOST TO HEAVEN

On the steps of the Castle Church Tilman von Rothenau kicked aside a leaf of lettuce. Hundreds of feet
overhead towered a Gothic spire, and to the boy, whose
upbringing had been pious and reverent, the shaft
seemed a signpost to heaven.

On the street not far away a wagon or cart sometimes rumbled over the paving stones of the Coswigerstrasse, headed out across the Elbe. When there was no
sound of hooves or iron rims he could hear the quiet
gurgle of flowing water, where the currents of the Faule
Bach and the Rische Bach joined at the mill-race. Once
they had ground the grain at the town mill, they flowed
out through a grill to fill the moat.

A trio of pigeons scampered away, within crumb's

throw. On the steps of the church a hunchback with a basket of apples sat begging for his living. Behind him massive oaken doors with fittings of wrought iron guarded the gold and silver relics that lay within.

Inside the narthex, candles flickered as brightly as stars in a darkened sky. At a tiny stand near the stairwell a wizened old woman tended a stock of candles. Largely out of habit and because he thought it a pleasant way to support the church, Tilman bought a candle, lit it, and added it to the score of others flaming in an iron rack before the image of the Virgin.

As his eyes grew accustomed to the light, he noted a display of devotional cards. He had seen them as a young boy in Torgau, but he had not seen any for a dozen years. What caught his eye now was not so much the wide range of saints from which one could enlist a patron (the Virgin herself, Saint Catherine, Jerome, Martin of Tours, Boniface, Gregory, Peter—in fact, any saint you could name) as the skillful printing which had gone into the cards. The printer's marks were largely from Paris and Strassburg, with three- and four-color printing that showed a fine sense of registry and inking. To do so careful a job on a block half the size of an ordinary page certainly would not be impossible, but the effort would demand skilled artisans and increase the price.

He had not until this moment noticed the little

cluster of pilgrims gathered in the far corner—a middle-aged man and his wife, well dressed in damask and broadcloth, two twittering housemaids, probably from the outlying villages, and an old woman bent with arthritis.

Against the dark wall he could make out the black robes of a Dominican, chatting as proudly about the noble church as if he had built it himself. "Come along, young man," the Dominican called. "You seem a stranger and I take it you'd like to see the relics."

Tilman brushed back the forelock that continually fell over his brow. True, he *had* come to see the relics. Yet he was not eager to succumb to the sales talk of a monk, particularly one in the habit of a Dominican. Even as the party of pilgrims pushed its way up the worn limestone of the steps, the monk began his lecture. He could scarcely have been out of his twenties, with a fluent tongue and impatient enthusiasm. There was an air of assurance in his manner that was belied by his scant number of years.

He seemed to pay more attention to the middle-aged man, who, it was revealed, was a lawyer, than to all the others combined, perhaps hoping for a large contribution. "As you have heard, the Castle Church is among the noblest sanctuaries in our land. Our gracious duke, the elector Johann Fredrick, has spent his whole lifetime and his whole fortune to make this the finest shrine in Germany. Except for two or three cathedrals, he has succeeded."

As Tilman scanned the gallery, he was quite willing to agree. He had read much about the Schlosskirche, and now that he could look out through the open balustrade into the great nave, he was not disappointed. The majesty of the vaulting, the ornate limestone altar and pulpit, the elegance of the hanging galleries, the intricacy of the carvings, the antique glass with sunlight dancing through, the artful attention to the smallest detail—all this filled him with awe.

"The view you have here," the guide said, pointing through the stone tracery to the nave below, "many pilgrims consider the most moving in our land. In the gold monstrance there in the foreground, outlined against the high altar, you see the queen of all the treasures. This is a thorn from Christ's very crown, brought to Constantinople by St. Helena and acquired by the duke from a church in Ravenna. If you examine it carefully, you can still note the stain of blood where it pierced the brow of our Savior." The girls crowded close, crossed themselves, and then made room for the others. Tilman's eyes wandered around the cathedral, to the long galleries supported artfully along the sides and back of the church, glittering with gold and silver reliquaries and with glass showcases. He noticed the worn stones of the pavement, showing the passing of thousands of feet.

"How many sacred objects are there?" asked one of the girls.

"There are 22,416, Fräulein. But don't try to count them. A score or more are always at the goldsmiths for a new fitting or case. Of course, the duke is always adding to the collection, too, either from his own travels or through his agents. If you view them all, and if your visit had been made on All Saints Day, you would have indulgences for 1,972,406 years and 38 days."

"But this isn't All Saints."

"Unfortunately, no. Nonetheless you will still gain remission in purgatory for more than 500,000 years, which is still enough, don't you think?"

The little party of visitors moved from case to case and from shrine to shrine. As a background the walls were finished with frescoes and mosaics and canvases, which themselves were treasures. As the brass plaque in the entry had suggested, Tilman searched out the trademarks of the artists, chiefly Jan Mabuse, Jacopo dei Barbari, Albrecht, Dürer, and Lucas Cranach.

Cranach seemed to have done a vast share of the work with his own brush, and for the first time Tilman began to realize just how great the artist's standing really was. No wonder the duke had presented him so glorious a house and showered him with commissions and even added the apothecary, for extra income.

Though the walk up the steps had been an easy one, Tilman moved his left thigh only with noticeable effort. His pallid face still showed how seriously he had been injured, and occasionally, if his step was too quick or too far, he felt a tinge of pain down into the great muscle of the thigh.

"Here," the young Dominican went on, warming with enthusiasm as he noticed the impression his words made, "you see four hairs from the head of Our Lady. Note the delicacy of the fiber and the softness of the color. These are of great antiquity and were long revered in a shrine in Alexandria. They were brought to Spain at the time the Moors overran Egypt."

The youth from Torgau had seen many holy objects in his life, whenever the priests carried them through the streets in the Corpus Christi parade, but he had never in his wildest dreams imagined there could be so many and such unusual relics in a single church.

The pilgrims gave due respect to all the holy objects, especially those most intimately connected with the life of our Lord and his church. Tilman found himself in a warm and mystical mood. His thoughts turned toward his mother and the stories she had recounted on the hearth about Jesus at Cana, Bethlehem, Bethsaida, and Nazareth.

His emotions welled up within him to a point where he could imagine no life quite so holy as one spent in the company of the relics, where they would always be a part of the mind and the heart. In fact, if the monk had asked him to consider seeing the abbot and spending his life in a cowl, he might well have agreed.

Each object was worth seeing, though the effect might have been more impressive if the lesser ones had been stored, or perhaps placed in outlying churches which could boast none of their own. The party viewed in turn a portion of bread from the Last Supper, a patch of cloth from the robe of John the Baptist, a vial of milk from the breasts of the Blessed Virgin Mary, a gold-incrusted skeleton of one of the Holy Innocents, a wisp of straw from the manger at Bethlehem, a strand of hair from the beard of our Redeemer, a fragment of root from Moses' burning bush, a little bottle of Christ's tears when he had wept over Jerusalem, a shard of the Wise Men's frankincense, and a swatch of the Christ Child's swaddling clothes.

The pilgrim band was small and was not influenced by the excitement as large crowds are. Everyone grew quiet and meditative. Only the monk kept the flow of conversation light and airy and the pilgrims moving from one gallery to another.

The lawyer and his wife appeared only partially impressed, unless it was perhaps that their age and maturity kept down their ebullience. Tilman, in fact, wondered why they had come at all, since in their lack of enthusiasm they seemed more like woodcutters trudging through the forest with a load of faggots than like meditative pilgrims.

As the party entered another gallery the lawyer asked a quiet question. "Tell us something of the indulgences, Frater. At Wurzburg we know the Castle Church not so much for its architecture or its holy things as for the spot where Martin Luther posted his theses nearly three years ago. Has he not put an end to the veneration of relics, or do we hear wrongly?"

The monk flushed angrily and with a flutter of the hand tried to regain his composure. "We do not even like to mention the name of that heretic in these sacred surroundings. Still, perhaps I can answer you and yet not offend my Maker. To be sure, the hundreds who once crowded this shrine now no longer come, especially the townfolk. The effrontery of that beast in denying the power of these holy things! He discards even the indulgences, the Pontiff's written promise of forgiveness!"

They were standing before a shrine in an alcove. An oil painting nearly life size showed the risen Savior ascending into heaven, with the figures of the disciples gathered around. The stone where Jesus stood was real granite, neatly fitted into the wall and shaped into the canvas. It reputedly was brought from the Holy Land by St. Peter.

The lawyer appeared quiet and imperturbable, with a knowing face and tinges of gray at his temples. "What about the elector? Does he still offer indulgences?"

"Yes, good sir, he does. I really ought to say he no longer advertises them, but I am happy to say they are still for sale, from the woman at the stall. Three years ago it was our biggest source of income, and needless to say, this church in all its glory would not stand as a tribute to the Good Lord if it were not for the indulgence money."

"Then the elector is opposed to the indulgences? He sides with Brother Martin?"

"No, not exactly. He is opposed to sending good German gold across the Alps. He does not wish to help build St. Peter's. But if the Germans want a written certificate that their sins are forgiven, instead of an oral promise, he is still willing to sell one."

By now Tilman was feeling extremely tired. His hip ached to the point where he occasionally had to sit on a bench to rest, as did the old lady with arthritis. Before long he would have to withdraw from the tour and leave the remainder of the sightseeing for another day. Still, the turn of the conversation had quickened his interest. Certainly there were heretics and differences

of opinion even in the church. Yet never in his life had
he seen one monk so bitter toward another.

"Tell me, brother," chimed in Tilman, "will the Good
Father in Rome do nothing to silence Luther? Surely he
should not be allowed to deceive the faithful, even
though the faithful are but simple peasants and shep-
herds."

"In another year or two the storm will have subsided,
you may be quite certain. Already there are rumors the
pontiff has issued a bull to condemn Brother Martin"—
he spoke the word brother with scorn so derisive he almost spat—"and by winter Luther will either recant
or perish."

The lawyer was not ready to let the subject lapse,
though for the moment the monk seemed eager to return to the script of his tour. "Isn't this a fight between
the Dominicans and the Augustinians? I've never seen
an Augustinian who disagreed with Brother Martin,
nor a Dominican who agreed."

The monk was being pinned to the wall, and though
he may have admired the skilled arguing of the lawyer
he nonetheless hated the inquisition. His face revealed
mounting anger, and if he held his tongue somewhat, it
was not because he wanted to but because he feared he
might lose a sizable contribution if he did not.

"Unfortunately the Augustinians have listened too

attentively to their little professor. In fact, even a few weaker Dominicans have cast off their habit and left the monastery. But this does not make Luther right. If the duke had taken a firm stand and supported the archbishop, the issue would have been settled long ago. Now all Germany is aflame."

"Excuse me," said Tilman, whose ears were filled with the quiet anger of the argument, "I'm but a simple country boy from Torgau and had not even heard the name of Luther until I came to Wittenberg. What does he teach, to be such a heretic?"

The monk smiled at his innocence. "Sometimes I think it wiser not to repeat error. But Doctor Martin has already written so much and preached so much and taught so much it is no longer possible to silence him easily. He thinks we should have more preaching, and less of the mass. He prefers the German language to Latin, as if Latin were not good enough, even if it was used by Jerome and Augustine. He wants singing in the church, not just by the monks but by the whole congregation."

"Is that bad?"

"It hasn't been done. It makes the people think they're as important as the priest, and when they get uppish ideas they will soon think they can conduct their own services. He wants Communion offered with both bread and wine, instead of bread alone. Huss was burned for that heresy. He wants no private masses for the royalty, and none for the souls of the dead. He wants fewer fast days. In God's eyes, he says it makes no difference whether a priest marries. Worst of all, he insists that a man is saved by faith. Not by giving alms, not by doing good works, not by buying indulgences, not by going on pilgrimages, not by saying the rosary, not by confessing his sins. By faith alone! As if the saints and apostles can't help!"

"And he preaches this in public?"

"Preaches, teaches, and writes. The university is one vast beehive of heresy."

The scuffling of boots on the paving stones brought a halt to the conversation. Along the portico a well-dressed burgher strode purposefully toward the pilgrims. His voice was at once familiar, though he spoke softly within the revered walls of the church.

"Tilman! It's good to see you on your feet and even climbing stairs." Cranach glanced from face to face. "Ah, Brother Francis. I hope you're explaining how much more artistic Cranach is than Barbari." There was a teasing glint in his eyes.

"Good day, Meister Lucas." The monk's tone was icy.

"Why so hostile, pray? You still have a few pilgrims and that's better than none."

The monk could no longer hold his tongue, and he

spoke with bitterness. "Without men like you, Meister Lucas, these disturbances in the church would pass quickly. The duke would yield, if he stood alone. But you—a court painter, a town councilman, a man of wealth and influence, a property owner! If you withdrew your support, people would attend the service of the mass once more, and the pope would again be honored as the prince of the church."

The color rose in Cranach's cheeks and he opened his lips to reply, but the syllable he had started did not come out. Instead he turned to Tilman. "Come, son," he said quietly. "I have found a place for you at Melchior's, until you can travel again. We have much to discuss."

Tilman pulled himself up from the bench and nodded politely to the rest of the party. His leg hurt, and he was not unhappy the tour had been interrupted. Basically, he sympathized with Brother Francis, but he also had to admire Cranach for his strong but quiet stand, which he was coming to realize was sometimes more useful than a strident argument. With Cranach a step ahead, he limped toward the stairwell.

CHAPTER FIVE

THE WITCH-DUCKERS

The single day Tilman had planned to spend in the electoral town of Wittenberg had now turned into a month. Although the scar in his abdomen had become hard and firm, Dr. Pergesius encouraged him to wait six more weeks before setting out for Mainz. In the ten days he had spent under Melchior's roof, plump Lotte Klein had mothered him and plied him with blueberry cakes and chicken soup.

Gradually his cheeks filled out again and his skin assumed the ruddy color of youth. He rather liked Lotte and Melchior, who, although simpler folk than their Cranach in-laws, were also more human. Dumpy little Lotte faithfully lit her candle to the Virgin each morning at the chapel of the Franciscans, and hard-

working Melchior habitually accepted far more manuscripts than he could hope to set in type unless he put
in long hours by candlelight.

On a morning in late August, Tilman worked as
usual in the print shop. The rain had come down
heavily during the night, and the waters were racing
through the channels of the Rische Bach and Faule
Bach, much to the delight of the town miller, who had
suffered a dry summer and had said more than his
share of prayers for rain.

In the shop Tilman took a hand wherever he was
needed. Since the brothers had taught him so much Latin
and German, he was most useful as a compositor and
proofer. To run the press was normally the job of one
apprentice and a journeyman, and demanded a degree
of strength, but did not require the kind of education
and training needed for typesetting.

Melchior was a good enough printer to know that
his workers needed a change from time to time, and
Tilman most of all. If he was to learn all the facets
of turning out a book, he should try his hand at everything: setting the type, locking up the frame, laying out
the sequence, registering the tympan, inking the
platen, operating the press, drying the sheets, and
sewing the gatherings.

What did surprise Melchior was how much Tilman

already knew. Though the monks at Torgau had not taught him the whole trade, from manuscript to printed book, what they had taught was of a high caliber. In inking and rolling the platen, for example, he was far more skilled than anyone in the shop, even Melchior himself, and he had learned some tricks about the making of ink that produced a blacker and quicker drying imprint, with less of the lampblack soaking through.

With the air so damp that particular morning, the press ordinarily would have taken a rest. The day was too warm to build a fire, but too wet for the ink to dry at its best. Melchior should have assigned all hands to composing or gathering or cutting, but the duke's order was so urgent and the demand from the booksellers so pressing that he felt he might lose the whole edition if he did not save every hour and day he could.

Tilman suggested he be allowed to experiment with a two-color frontispiece, bearing the title *Address to the German Nobility* in black, and the colophon of the printer in royal blue. He had juggled the ingredients of the blue for days, and had finally come up with a brilliant color that printed nearly as well as did the brighter water-based inks used for woodcuts.

Melchior was so pleased he suggested Tilman and an apprentice run several hundred copies through the press. Together they decided to print two colors from a single impression. The apprentice was handling the lever. Tilman alternately inked the black title and the blue colophon.

The effort went so well that Melchior extended the run in color to five hundred copies, knowing full well that an extra page or two of color was worth at least ten groschen at the book stalls. With Tilman's method the extra cost in labor was no more than a few pfennigs. The other apprentice kept busy hanging the printed sheets to dry, while Melchior and a second journeyman set type directly into the chases.

The clouds still hung heavy over the land, as they do on an August day that signals the end of summer. The trees dripped from the night's rain, and though the cobblestones were partly dry, the sky looked as if another downpour might begin any moment.

With four hundred copies already through the press, Melchior had to decide whether to move the racks into the storage loft, which would mean he could keep the press rolling for another four hundred copies, or shift his crew to gathering and collating. There was plenty of work to do; it was merely a question of timing. The hour was still early, though with the sun hidden he would have to go out and look at the clock in the city hall to be sure. He decided to continue the run as long as the blue ink lasted.

Over the steady creak of the press, no one paid any attention at first to the girl who burst through the door, banging it so loud it would have made anyone but a printer's devil jump with fright. Sometimes a house-maid did burst in, with a message from Lotte or a summons for Melchior. The men were used to paying scant attention.

This girl, however, was not to be overlooked. She threw her arms about so wildly and shouted so pite-ously, in a high-pitched voice, and looked so bedraggled that she obviously was not of the household of Melchior Klein.

She went directly to the little cluster of men at the press, pointing straight at Tilman. Through her tears it was hard to make out what she was trying to say. "It's *him* I want. The one who saved the Cranach boy. They told me he would be here."

The men were so startled they hardly knew what to answer. It took a minute before the words made sense. By this time Melchior had joined the circle, trying to determine what it was all about. Tilman recognized her as the pretty girl he had seen at the market stall.

Her skirts were stained with mud, as if she had not only been splashed but tumbled into a puddle. Her black hair was wet, hanging in ringlets close against her cheeks. In spite of her tears she was attractive.

"My mother! They're going to duck her for a witch. Can't you do something?"

"Calm down, girl," came Melchior's knowing voice. "Where? Who is your mother?"

"The Widow Tannenlohe. At Kronberg. I'm her daughter Ingi."

"What makes you think they will do something so drastic? First they need a court order."

"You don't know the villagers, sir. They act first and think second. I overheard the priest and the wood-cutter, plotting. Hurry! Someone must help! No one in the village will lift a finger to save her."

The girl began to make considerable sense, but to a businessman like Melchior, to whom time meant money, the need was not clear-cut. "Can't you get the town guard? Can't you speak to a councilman and have the bailiff sent?"

"There's not time! She may be dying. What I need is someone who can run swiftly, who can slow them down, until their tempers cool. And if Tilman could save a boy from a stag, he can save my mother."

With this for an incentive Tilman von Rothenau looked appealingly at his boss. He edged toward the door, not knowing what to do, yet realizing he did not want to ignore a maiden in distress.

"Where do you live, girl?" Melchior ordered. "Which house in the village?"

"It's just beyond the church. The first house on the left, with wattle and thatch."

"You hear that, Tilman? Just beyond the church. And Kronberg is the first village on the way to Torgau. Only four miles out, on the left bank of the Elbe, and a few hundred paces up the hill. There's a windmill on top, and you can see it a mile away . . . How's the side? Think you can run?"

"Yes, Master Melchior."

"It's not too far. Stay with the woman until I get there. The girl and I will take the wagon and follow you. It'll take us ten minutes to hitch up and by then you'll be halfway there. Take the path from the Elstertor and you'll beat us. With the horses we'd better stay on the Elbgasse."

The girl lost her look of frantic anxiety, now that she had found help. Tilman raced through the gate, threaded his way through the winding turns of the Burgermeistergasse, and darted across the grazing land inside the town wall. Ahead he could see the massive tower of the Elstertor. A guard on the ramparts seemed rather sleepy in the mid-morning fog.

In a minute Tilman's boots had left the rough paving-stones, pounded the floor of the bridge, and then headed for open country on the sandy roadway. He was not running at full speed, for he knew by experience he could conserve his strength, in the long run, by slightly slowing his pace. He did not even feel pain in the groin and ran effortlessly. Herders and goose girls greeted him cheerily as he passed, but he jogged past in silence. Now that the windmill was in sight, he wondered what he would find.

The girl had been fairly explicit. Tannenlohe. An odd name for Saxony. And where was the girl's father? Off with the Army? And how had she discovered Tilman?

The more he thought, the more he grew confused. He couldn't believe he was racing through the country-side to save a woman from witch-hunters. If they still believed in witches, these Kronbergers were far more uninformed than he had thought. Torgau hadn't burned a witch for a generation.

The cluster of barns and cottages around the common loomed closer and closer. Across the river he thought he could see Melchior's wagon, between clumps of trees, still a good mile or two away. Pigs grunted and ducks quacked as he trotted past, pushed aside as if in the wake of a boat.

Near the pond Tilman saw a group of villagers, rais-ing their fists in anger and talking so excitedly that the buzz of their voices sounded as loud as the tramp of his boots. He quickened his gait and ran to the common.

The mill fronted the road, with a millrace leading up to the pond. Just where the waters tumbled into the

race, where the wooden weir could be raised and low-
ered to control the flow, the townsfolk had roped a chair
onto a long ashen pole and were busy tying down a
shrieking woman.

Tilman, breathless, dashed up to the woman, yelling
he knew not what except that he was making a great
deal of commotion, and took his stand, like a gander
hissing to protect its gosling. While he jeered at the
crowd he reached for his knife and cut the woman's
bindings.

From the angle of the pole, it was quite clear that
Frau Tannenlohe soon would have been swung over
the channel and been thoroughly immersed. As in the
usual test for witchcraft, if she drowned she proved herself innocent. But if she could swim her way to the
surface, with chair, ropes, and all, surely Satan himself
must be giving her the strength.

The woman's arms bled a little from the jabbing of
the sticks, where the villagers had probed for the devil's
mark. Although the crowd quieted a trifle when Tilman
burst into their midst, there were still hoots and cat-
calls. The poor woman trembled in every limb; three
young children wept unconsolably near the mill.

The crowd was not large, Tilman noticed, and it was
made up mostly of women. There could scarcely be
more than twenty, not counting those who stood beyond

the churchyard, as if they did not want to miss the spectacle but at the same time did not want to be counted among the perpetrators.

No one opposed the youth, however raucous their shouts. For a minute or two, Tilman expected a real brawl as they argued the right and wrong of what they were doing. "Shame!" he said, when the crowd settled down and his words could be heard, "Shame! Don't you know you can't try a witch without a legal writ? Who's your leader, anyway?"

The peasant wives looked disconcertedly from face to face, hoping the woodcutter or the wagonmaker would stand forth and argue their cause. But it appeared they had no champion.

"What is she guilty of, anyhow, the Widow Tannenlohe? Has she hexed your menfolk or robbed your wombs? Has she brought floods to your fields or mildew to your hay?"

One buxom woman in a dirty smock gathered her courage. She spoke quickly and sharply, like a jaybird. "She put a spell on the cattle, that's what she done. My Mousey and Spotty was due to calf next month, and they dropped their calves, dead. The widow was right in the wood lot when it happened."

"It couldn't be from the dry summer, could it? Dusty fodder, too much heat, disease? It had to be a witch?"

"It's not just that, boy. You couldn't understand. You're not one of us. You don't even got a good Wittenberg accent. Look at that birthmark. If that's not a devil's touch, I never seen one."

"A fishwives' tale. If everyone with a birthmark were a sorcerer, winter would be summer, and snow, dust!"

The shock of surprise had now faded, and the women pressed forward, eager to resume the attack. The widow Tannenlohe crouched behind her protector, still trembling, but casting a worried look toward her children. From behind the crowd a lean, beak-nosed hunter suddenly walked up, and for an instant Tilman expected that both he and the widow would wind up in the pond.

The gamekeeper wore a loose leather vest, with a brace of grouse slung in a net across his back. In his hands was an uncocked crossbow and a handful of bolts, carried loosely. "Don't be too hard on the villagers, laddie," he counseled, in an easygoing way. "Life is hard on the land, and heaven knows they can't afford to lose a calf."

The women did not know whether to count the gamekeeper on their side or Tilman's. He acted like a country philosopher, eager to explain what was happening but hardly one to take action. Tilman was relieved to see that the hunter was peaceful. Across the fields echoed the clatter of hooves and the sounds of chickens scurrying before the wagon. Melchior and the girl bore down on the village at full gallop.

The scolding housewife was not yet satisfied. "Why does she gather all that saffron and cook her greens with dill, if she's not a witch? Anyone knows that's what witches eat."

At this the widow Tannenlohe found her voice, though she was still quaking from the ordeal. "You know as well as I, Frau Hutter. Ingi sells the saffron at market. The dill we eat because we like it. Is there any crime in that?"

Now the wagon whirled to a stop beside the mill. Melchior tied the reins to a willow and ran toward the pond. It was not often a wagon stopped at Kronberg, or even passed through, since it was off the high road. The villagers ceased their chatter to examine its owner.

Meanwhile the gamekeeper talked quietly to Tilman. "That was a brave thing to do, lad. I was just coming up from the marsh or I'd have pitched in sooner. By the way, I'm from Wittenberg, too. Reinhard Zillerthal. I'm the town miller, thanks to the duke and my grandfather to whom the duke's grandfather gave the mill."

"I thought I'd seen you at mass in the Schlosskirche. But what are you doing here?"

"Well, I guess I'm not a very good miller. I have three helpers to keep the wheels grinding, and I have rather an aversion to flour. Being royal miller has its rights, you know—gaming, fishing, a free stall at the market, exemption from most taxes."

"In that vest you look like a poacher. Tell me, why do the village folk hate this woman so? Do they really think she's a witch?"

"No. They don't. But you've got to feel sorry for them. Taxes are high, and there's never any excitement. Every year they pay a tenth of their barley and chickens and cheese and vegetables just for Kirchensteuer, to support the monks and the church. They can't hunt or fish. They've got little to eat but dried beans and carp and coarse bread. They owe the court fifteen days' labor every year. Their cottages are damp and dark, and they're not much better off than serfs."

"Can't they get jobs in town?"

"They don't know a trade, most of them. Just farming. A witch hunt always stirs up excitement. So what if there is a law against it! The womenfolk still think they believe in witchcraft—passing a law won't eliminate it. Besides, the real trouble is over there, against the stone fence. Until people like Brother Heidrich are shut up, there'll be a witch hunt every month."

Tilman looked sharply at the monk outside the nearby churchyard. Standing there beside the swineherd and the woodcutter was the monk who had tried to steal his Aldine prayer book in the sickroom. He remembered that many outlying villages had no priest of their own and were served by the monasteries in town.

"He's a mean one, Heidrich," said Reinhard. "When a poor old woman's got nothing but a goat and a cottage, he'll still demand his tenth year after year. If she doesn't have crops to share he'll threaten to take the goat. He's done it too. Then she has nothing left—no milk, no cheese, no meat, no money."

"Do you think he's behind the witch hunt?"

"I wouldn't be surprised. If Frau Tannenlohe perished as a witch, the inheritance would not pass to the children. It would go to the church. There's not much— just a swampy patch of land and the cottage. Maybe a few goats and chickens. Of course the monastery would be expected to farm out the children, but what really happens is that they wind up as streetwalkers and roustabouts. Once the property goes to the church, that's the end of it. The church loses interest in the children."

While Tilman and Reinhard talked, Melchior and Ingi had rounded up her mother and her three brothers and sisters. They started to move across the shady lane toward the cottage as the sunshine broke through the clouds and flitted across the pond.

"You'll be quite safe, Frau Tannenlohe," Melchior said, soothing her. "If I thought it would do any good, you could stay with us in town for a few days. But now they're quite harmless, these women. Once I talk to two or three of the men, they'll have to protect you, or face hanging. Besides, running away wouldn't solve it. Someone's got to keep an eye on your garden and the goats and chickens."

As they entered the gate, the crowd dispersed. Heidrich sullenly trudged through the soggy sand of the street, kicking up debris with his open-toed sandals. Ten feet away, without halting his stride, he raised his finger toward Tilman. "If you stand in my way just once more," he said, raising his voice so little he might have been saying a cheery good morning, "I'll see you die in purgatory. You and the girl and her mother and the whole kit and caboodle of you."

Tilman had been so carefully reared to respect a man of God, especially one who had taken vows of poverty, chastity, and obedience, that he hardly knew what to answer. But Herr Klein had heard every word, and was not as intimidated as Tilman.

"Heidrich, you preach one more sermon against witchcraft, you allow one more test without the writ of a court, you bother this family in any way, and I personally will see you unfrocked. In fact, if any Tannenlohe is hurt or injured, I swear I'll see you hang on the gallows, even if you think you're exempt from a civil court!"

The monk spat contemptuously into a puddle and did

not deign to answer. He continued down the lane, swung across the turf of the churchyard, and slammed the vestry door.

Tilman stayed outside with the huntsman. Reinhard spoke. "Tilman, I think Heidrich has designs on that girl, Ingi, who is the cleverest in the village and prettiest, too. But from the look she gave you when they drove up, you're St. George and Charlemagne and Emperor Constantine all rolled into one." He paused a moment. "Tell you what. There's probably not much to eat in the house, and they'd welcome some meat." He took a pair of game birds from his pouch. "Give them these, from me. I'll shoot another on the way home." With that, he nodded companionably, heading back for the willow thickets along the bottomlands.

"Wait, Herr Zillerthal. Will I get to see you in Wittenberg? I didn't even get to thank you."

"*Nichts zu danken,* son, nothing to thank for." He cranked back the metal string of the crossbow and loaded his weapon. "Any time. If you can't find me at the mill I'm probably out with a bow or a rod . . . God bless!"

"Thank you, sir," said Tilman. "God bless!"

CHAPTER SIX

THE COURT
OF THE ELECTOR

Had it been a market day, Tilman surely would have detoured through the square, in hopes of seeing Ingi. In a way he was glad there was no market. The book in his hands was worth at least three gulden, carefully wrapped in foolscap to keep any grease or sweat from the binding. To dillydally at the market with so valuable a book would have bothered his conscience.

It was nearly the end of August, and the lindens that grew along the Faule Bach, on the far side of the square, were dropping the first of their winged nuts. At the crowns the outer leaves had taken on a shade of yellow. The autumn rains would soon bring them skidding to the cobblestones.

Tilman clomped across the wooden bridges of the Faule Bach and the Rische Bach, only a stone's throw apart where they began to rush together to form the millrace, and turned down the Schlossgasse.

His face was fuller than it had been for months, thanks to the excellent cooking of Lotte Klein, and he was impatient to set out for Mainz. Doctor Pergesius must think him a starved weakling, to order so long a convalescence.

A youngster with a hoop, the rim from a large wagon, darted thoughtlessly in his path, but Tilman gave him ample room. This was no time to trip over curbing and splash into the stream, book and all.

Ahead he could see the huge quadrangle of the castle. Although the view was somewhat blocked by the mill, one could see the towers from anywhere in town, or, for that matter, from miles away in the countryside. On the north the quadrangle was bounded by the Schlosskirche, with its massive round tower reaching hundreds of feet in the air, and the ornate, smaller tower that rose from the transept.

On the east the castle was walled in by two-story buildings which housed the various offices of the state: the armory, the customs house, the guards' quarters, the stables, and the bakehouse. The palace fronted the south and west, where it could drink in the winter sun and air, and where the duke could look out over the moat and the river.

Tilman clutched the book tightly in his hand, went through the walkway behind the Schlosskirche, and presented himself to the armed guard at the gate. "I have a book to deliver to His Grace, as ordered from the print shop Klein."

The guard grunted, swatted at a fly buzzing around his ear, and pointed through the courtyard. "Over there. Second floor."

Tilman scooted through. Although one could get a casual glimpse of the courtyard from the windows of the church, the area was larger and more pleasant than he remembered. Against the stone walls grapes had been trained on trellises, to catch every ray of sunshine. The retaining wall between church and palace was green with ivy and ramblers, and in the middle of the pavement stood a pretty pool.

A youngster of two or three toddled around the low stone rim and was lured by the spouting statues of Triton and four fishes. The sparkle of huge goldfish swimming below was a great temptation, and he stuck one pudgy little leg over the rim and into the water.

"Whoa there, sonny!" Tilman caught him by the arm and pulled him away. The boy looked disappointed, though a bit too startled to protest. "Ponds are for fish. Not for little boys. Where's your mommy, anyway?"

"Up there."

A cluster of potted ferns at the base of the statue blocked the view, and Tilman took a step or two backward, keeping one hand on the precious package and the other on the youngster. Until this moment he had not noticed the courtier sitting with a wooden flute beneath a carefully cropped almond tree.

The courtier rose to his feet and ambled leisurely toward the apprentice. "I must have dozed off," he commented. "If he had fallen in, there'd be the devil to pay." Tilman wondered which one of the court officials he was talking to, dressed not too carefully, however expensive the satin of his doublet. The chamberlain, perhaps, or the steward, the court poet or the legal counselor.

His hair was rather unkempt, especially the beard, which flowed out like a circle from ear to ear, but was trimmed off neatly from the front of the face, except for a waxed mustache. He moved casually and appeared eager to help. He had the dreamy eyes of a poet.

"What have you there, apprentice?"

"A book, sir. I meant to leave it at the gate but the guard said to deliver it."

"What kind of book?"

"*The Address to the German Nobility*. Perhaps you've heard of it, sir. Herr Klein tells me it's quite well known."

"Perhaps I have." The courtier gave no sign of recognition. "They're printing so many these days it's hard to keep track. Those professors seem to keep writing them, and the printers keep printing them."

"I wouldn't know, sir. This was something special His Grace earnestly desired. We've gone to considerable trouble—a colored imprint and a special binding of kidskin. Lettered and embossed with gold leaf at the goldsmiths."

"Could I see it, please? Then I'd know whether I've read the book or not."

Tilman hesitated. "If it's not hurting your feelings, sir, I'd rather not. You see, it's all wrapped in foolscap, and I must be careful of fingerprints, until the elector sees it."

"You're quite right. He's a rather fussy old goat, and we'd hate to displease him. Tell me, what's the book about anyway?"

"I haven't read it all, sir. Just what I set in type or proofread. Lufft sold more than five thousand copies in a month. Since Klein had new matrices the elector asked him to reprint it, with one copy in kid, to send to his brother."

"It must be important. Tell me, what do you think of it—the parts you read, I mean?"

Tilman still clung to the hand of the toddler, who was growing bored with all this talk. Nonetheless the lad stood quiet now, watching a pair of sparrows taking their bath in the fountain. "It bothers me, sir. Mind you, I'm not a theologian. Far from it. But my mother did train me as a faithful believer, and I'm somewhat bothered."

The courtier smiled knowingly and toyed with the flute. "What in particular?"

"Almost everything. The church can't be as evil as Luther says. Maybe a pope or a bishop did have a child or a sticky finger, but one bad egg doesn't spoil the whole basket. There's a skeleton in every closet."

"You think the Medici and Borgia families were a credit to the Holy Office?"

Tilman's brow wrinkled, and the cleft in his chin firmed. He was not quite sure on which side the courtier stood, but he did seem to want Tilman's opinion. "I guess I don't really know. But these notions of Luther that any believer can read the Bible and that one cannot be saved by good works will split Mother Church wide open. Is that what he wants?"

"You seem to know more about the book than you thought. Are these ideas just Luther's?"

"No, not from what Master Melchior tells me. Master Lucas, too. The whole faculty seems to agree. Melanchthon, they say, and the law professor, what's his name— Schurf. Herr Cranach says Luther wrote the book only in jest, acting the 'court fool' to see what the response would be. But now the fire is lighted, and it's out of control."

"If you're really so opposed, perhaps you shouldn't be exposed to the argument."

"No, I've been to school, a good school — the Brothers of the Common Life in Torgau. A man who's been schooled can weigh and decide. It's the common folks I feel sorry for. They'll be the ones who are misled and will follow the Judas buck right into the slaughterhouse. Of course, I did make my mother a promise, on her deathbed, to hold fast to the faith. In days like these, and without my parents, it's not easy."

"You must be the lad who saved Master Lucas' boy."

"Yes, sir."

"The whole town talked about it. I'm glad to see you've recovered and have settled down in Wittenberg."

"It's not for long, sir. I was headed for Mainz, to learn the printing trade. The doctor says I'm to wait another month or two before I'm fit. Before the winter snows I'll be moving on. Lucas put me with his brother-in-law, so I wouldn't be wasting my time. Still, the whole town is in such an uproar, with the monks leaving the monasteries and all these students flooding to the university, I'll be glad to get out."

The courtier hitched up the buckskin buskins that had slipped down around his ankles. He twiddled a

moment with the wooden *Bockflöte,* trying to mimic
the curious twittering of the swallows. "The book goes
to the library. I haven't seen His Grace's secretary this
morning, Herr Spalatin, but he's almost always buried in
the folios up on the second floor." He nodded toward an
arched doorway.

Tilman pushed back the unruly mop of hair from his
brow and appeared confused.

"Come, I'll show you." The courtier was not a
young man, and he had traces of gray in his beard and
locks. Surely he must be in the good graces of the duke,
to judge from the giant emerald on his finger, Tilman
thought. The man trudged resolutely toward the entryway. The child tagged along hand in hand with Tilman.
The huge reception hall sparkled with warmth and
color, although Tilman got nothing more than a quick
impression of its glories: Grecian marble, Italian ter-
razzo, paintings, frescoes, tapestries, chandeliers.

They trod up the spiral staircase, and turned down
a long hall. "Normally the elector doesn't like those
who come to the library to use this entry, but I know
him rather well and I don't think he'll mind."

Tilman was so awe-struck by the majesty of the surroundings he could hardly keep up. The castle surpassed
even the majesty of the church. "Tell me, boy, does
Wittenberg still look like a little country town, with
muddy streets and garbage in the gutters and pigs run-

ning wild through the market?" The apprentice did not
at once know what to say. It was obvious his leg was
being pulled. The courtier continued, "At least we have
as good a castle and church as any in Germany."

The courtier grinned at the word *we*. At the end of
the hallway he quickly entered an arch. Across the long
room a bony-faced priest quickly rose to his feet, a
little awkward and with the look of a man who handles
himself as a scholar rather than an athlete. The older
man put his finger to his lips, winked an eye, and the
priest nodded. Tilman was engrossed in the glories of
the library to the point where he paid little attention to
his companions.

"This is Master Melchior's apprentice. He has a
book for His Grace. *The Address to the German Nobility*. I do suggest you handle it carefully, George, for
we wouldn't want any fingerprints on it before the
duke sees it." He winked again, then turned to Tilman.

"Apprentice, this is Herr Spalatin, the duke's chaplain
and secretary. The book will be safe with him."

Tilman clicked his heels together and bowed slightly.
He was far more interested in the magnificent trappings
of the library than in his hosts. Compared with the en-
trance hall the library was Spartan, and yet it was the
most magnificent library young Tilman had ever seen.
The half-timbered ceiling, in the plastered areas between the beams, was completely covered with frescoes

from the history of Rome, and the ornate stacks for books had griffons and unicorns carved into the uprights.

Although he was not nearly as old as the courtier, the librarian had an austere look. His cheeks were gaunt and his lips thin, and but for the darting sparkle of his eyes he might have been more at home as a hermit.

"Welcome, apprentice. We've been waiting for you, and for the book. The duke wants to get it off to his brother with the first coach. But what of the others he ordered? Are they ready?"

"Nearly, sir. Master Melchior ran ten plates early today. Then the bookbinder fell sick. No one else can handle kidskin quite so well. The others will be ready tomorrow. The ones in calf."

Spalatin thumbed through the octavo. His knowing fingers fondled the paper, testing its quality, and his eyes quickly ran over a page of type. He held the leather cover in sure but gentle hands, and his eyes lighted up with excitement. "This is truly a gift fit for a king. I'm sure His Grace will be most pleased."

"Thank you, sir. I'm rather pleased with it myself, what little I did see. It's nearly as perfect as an Aldine, if I may say so."

"You know about Aldines, lad?" The monk's eyes seemed to pierce into his very thoughts.

"Yes, sir. My mother gave me one, a prayerbook. I've always wanted to be a printer, and she said if I could ever produce a book like that, I'd be a master among masters."

"She was right. Nobody makes them quite so well as Aldus. We have fifty or more right here in the library. Not all are out where the students can use them, of course, especially those with gilded bindings. But I must say this is as close to an Aldine as I've seen in Germany."

Tilman blushed almost as deeply as if he himself had been the proprietor of the print shop. "I'm sure Master Melchior will be pleased."

The courtier broke into the conversation. "The boy tells me he's confused. He likes the binding and the printing but not the content. He thinks Luther should be more respectful."

Spalatin smiled, and on his gaunt face the effect was peculiar. His long, thin nose wrinkled as he laughed.

"Not even the doctors of theology know what it's all about. But they will. Every court in the land is talking about *The Address to the German Nobility*. In another month the disease will strike all Europe. You just watch!"

Tilman was not altogether happy about the chaplain's zeal. "Don't you think there's a chance that Luther is wrong?"

Spalatin guffawed. "He might be injudicious or naive or undiplomatic, but he's not wrong. These things have needed saying for centuries, and praise God we've got a monk with the courage to say them."

The courtier touched Tilman, who was obviously embarrassed and had turned to leave. "The easiest way out," he said, "is through the door at the end. That will take you right out to the battlements and the street. By the way, if you ever have a free hour, you're quite welcome to use the library. The students do, and the elector would be happy to have you."

"Thank you, sir. Thank you." He bowed and departed.

The courtier stood tugging at his beard, and pulled once more at the calfskin boot that kept slipping down over his ankle. "There's one Wittenberger Luther still has to convert, George. If he can convince the thoughtful kind, like that boy, he'll have his Reformation won."

Out on the battlements Tilman caught his breath and smiled wryly. "Mother Mary!" he exclaimed, half in disgust, half in excitement. "That ring! With the royal crest! It must have been the elector himself!"

CHAPTER SEVEN

TURK'S ATTACK

Tilman von Rothenau dipped his finger into the font of holy water, made the sign of the cross, and genuflected. The water felt cold, after a cold night in a cold chapel. It was cold enough to distract his meditations. He wondered whether the Virgin would intercede for him. Those who came to church, he had always been taught, should concentrate so fully on their sins and on God's forgiveness that they had no time for noticing whether the holy water was cold.

For a September day it was unusually cold. There had been a hint of frost the night before, and in the tiny limestone chapel of the Franciscans the air was always cool, even at noon on the hottest day of July.

The two-block walk from the print shop had been just enough to warm the blood, and though it meant rising at five-thirty rather than six, when the rest of the household got up, Tilman made it a practice to attend matins.

For one thing, he was more than thankful about his injury. A little more loss of blood or a wound an inch or two higher through the intestine, Dr. Pergesius explained, and he would not be alive. But at seventeen Tilman was not so much preoccupied with his close call as with the pure pleasures of living. He counted his blessings. He'd had the kind of education that was rare, for his day, even though it had stopped at seventeen. He knew as much about a skilled trade as many a thirty-year-old journeyman. His master was kind, his mistress a fine cook, and had it not been for years of dreaming and scheming he might have found Wittenberg a good substitute for Mainz.

One thing about the town that bothered him was the Reformation. For the moment he was not sure whether this was a problem just in Wittenberg or whether all Germany was being infected by Luther. All this accent on preaching and singing and talking about salvation without good works. The antagonism toward priest and bishop and pope. Where would it all end? No matter how sincere Brother Martin's motives, it was quite clear to Tilman that Luther was a renegade, a renegade whom the townspeople supported for self-ish motives, and that the whole lot of them were in the same class as the pagans who once sacked Rome.

The chapel was empty except for a goose girl from the market, a couple of arthritic old women whose joints obviously pained them when they kneeled, and a wrinkled old artisan. Before the high altar the Franciscans performed their ritual, marching silently, chanting reverently, almost unaware of the few who came to share the service.

Among all the churches in Wittenberg Tilman thought none so churchlike as that of the Franciscans. The popular churches were the Stadtkirche, which a few old-timers still called St. Mary's, and the Schlosskirche. One stood just off the market square, in the center of town, and the other directly inside the Coswigertor, close to the cottages outside the gate.

Wittenberg also boasted the three chapels of the monks: the Franciscans, the Antonites, and the Augustinians. None of these really encouraged the townsfolk to share in their offices, but at the same time no abbot would have considered excluding anyone who wanted to worship. All three chapels had at least a gallery where outsiders were welcome. Services at the old chapel of the Antonites were irregular, with the brothers—only a few—living outside the walls in priories. Hardly anyone ever walked across the fields to the Augustinians, near the Elstertor, especially since Luther had been invited to preach regularly in the Stadtkirche.

It was not strange that Tilman went to church at the Franciscan chapel, if one considered his background. What he had learned at his mother's knee and the fine understanding he had developed with the Brothers of the Common Life he never would lose. He understood the monks and loved their rituals. Perhaps for this reason he felt more at home with the Franciscans than in the Stadtkirche, where Lotte and Melchior attended mass.

No one at the print shop except Melchior knew he went to mass daily. He did not deny it, but he usually described it as a morning walk, and let it go at that. He would not have minded the jibes of scurrilous apprentices or students, any more than he minded their jokes about the peach fuzz on his cheeks or his oversized Adam's apple. However, he saw no advantage in advertising his piety.

The stone was cold against his knees, and even though his crossed fingers clutched the rail before him, he shivered. He was only vaguely aware of the usual paraphernalia of the service and the odor of burning camphor, the candlewicks guttering in the draft, the musty odor of centuries-old limestone.

Somehow, as the son of a Freiherr, as the son of a squire who had been knighted, he thought it his obligation to carry on the traditions of his predecessors. Even if some church-goers longed for something new, even if they wanted to hear a sermon in German and not just the old ritual in Latin, even if they wanted to sing and not just listen to the chant of the priests, he was quite content with the old. People of quality and understanding had to help save the old treasures even when the simple and unlearned pleaded for a change.

For Tilman each act of the mass was somehow a prop to his faith. The ringing of the bells at the consecration, the elevating of the host, the color of the chasuble, the cut of the alb—all warmed his heart. The censing of the acolytes, the lighting of the candles, the unveiling of the statuary, helped remind him he was in the temple of God.

That he was in the presence of monks and not just parish priests also brought a pleasant reminder of the faith he had once learned at his own hearth. The austerely beautiful chanting of the plainsongs and the responses was something he missed in a parish church, and he was glad he had grown up at Torgau, not in a country parish beyond the reach of the monasteries.

In front of the altar old friar Tenzing, who looked not nearly as short and dumpy when he celebrated mass as he did at other times, sonorously chanted the *Gloria in excelsis,* echoed by a score of monks, proceeding step by step through the liturgy. He kissed the relic-bearing altar stone, broke the host, washing his fingers in symbolic ritual.

At the bell of consecration Tilman felt a chill of excitement run through his frame. He imagined himself beneath the cross of Calvary, facing the Lord of the universe just as surely as the friar gazed upon the corpus. *In, with,* and *through* his presence, according to the words of the ancient formula, the youth felt himself sharing his life with God.

Whatever the day brought he could face once he had been to mass. Tedious hours over the font, an aching back from the huge lever, a snub from one of the apprentices, an ache or pain, a disappointment, a sickness of heart, were cured by the mass. He would never give it up, Luther or no Luther, and he would have it, if you please, in its pristine form, just as he had learned it in Torgau.

The Franciscans received the benediction, blessed the officiant in turn, and after a silent prayer, marched one by one to the black cross inlaid in the marble predella, genuflected, and rhythmically retreated from the choir. As each knelt, he broke his silence and joined in the Great Hallel, *In exitu Israel,* as a kind of thanks for all God's gifts.

Tilman took in the ceremony with eyes and ears, remaining for some time on his knees. Even the old women were on their feet plodding out the doorway when he finally rose. His heart was filled with a great hallelujah, like that of the brothers. He bowed, crossed himself, and strode out into the dawning sunlight. The day was good and so was God, and he was glad to be alive.

Three blocks away on the town square the high-pitched angelus signalled the morning call to work. Fishwives threw open their shutters, haulers rumbled through the streets, butchers spread new sawdust beneath their counters and bakers lit their ovens.

High atop the spire of the Stadtkirche the little old couple in their tiny apartment, who doubled as bell-ringers and fireguards, stared down from the railing, peering out toward the rosy glow of the sunrise. In the market place below, everyone was hustling.

As usual Ingi Tannenlohe had arrived early and readied her stall. To be at the square at seven meant rising at five and trundling a two-wheeled cart four miles. On the south side of the market, facing the town hall, she had an ideal location, near one of the foot-bridges across the Faule Bach.

The leaves were completely yellow from the September frosts, a sign that winter was not far off. Ingi stacked the wooden trays of carrots and honey on the framework of the counters. The netted sacks of cabbage, beets, and leek were sorted out below, in a color-ful pile, and the more valuable of her wares, the balls of cheese and the boxes of hazelnuts and the wooden cage with four clucking hens, stayed right on the cart at the edge of the stall.

With her work almost finished, there was time to catch her breath. With a touch of winter in the air, the knitted leggings her mother had made were cozy, and her stocking cap not only held her curls in place but warmed her ears. Its faded red made her hair appear even darker and glossier.

Beyond Ingi's stall, beyond the fruits and vegetables, spread the fish market. Frau Schimmelpfennig, the hawker whose voice could pierce to the farthest doorways and whose passion for arguing kept her tongue constantly in motion, was already hard at work. A good share of her eels and carp and pike she kept in wicker cages, dropping them with a short rope into the flowing waters of the millrace.

Here at the market the stream was under careful control, tumbling neatly through a cobblestone bed to supply power to the town mill and, in case of siege, drinking water. Flowing on a wooden aqueduct across the waters of the moat and through a grill in the wall, it got its water from the duke's fishpond, a short walk beyond the moat. However vulnerable the wooden aqueduct may have looked in time of war, not many enemies would have been so foolhardy as to sneak up under the grapeshot from the towers.

With the heat of the summer past, the bustle of shoppers sounded sprightlier than usual. The main artery through the town from the Elstertor to the Coswigertor, known at one end as the Collegiengasse and at the other as the Schlossgasse, lay just beyond the Faule Bach. Occasionally caravans of merchants, sometimes twenty wagons at a time, rumbled past the market.

The students had flocked back, too, for the new term, and the streets fluttered not only with the capes of the faculty but also with those of their charges. To keep them from trouble and to make them readily identifiable if they caused too much difficulty in the taverns or *Frauenhäuser,* the students were required to wear an identifying cape. Housewives jammed the market too, anxious to lay a good supply of beets and turnips in their root cellars before a killing frost raised prices.

Ingi could not have looked more content. This early in the morning she had already made two sales, always a sign of a good day's business. As the splotches of sunlight crawled up over the roofs of the town, glistening dully off the slate and not at all off the thatch, she hummed a little folk song about a journeyman homesick for Nürnberg and his sweetheart.

Off toward the church she heard a raucous scuffling and shouting. A market girl of long standing, she identified the troublemakers as students. They stumbled out crazily from the Bursa Mercury. Now that a new term was about to begin, they obviously had celebrated the last days of their freedom with too much wine-swilling.

She recognized their leader at once. He was Turk Stutzer, a hot-blooded Rhinelander and student of medicine. As a town character he was as notorious as Frau Schimmelpfennig. When he was drunk he was mean. In the spring he'd been jailed for kicking the child of a glazier. Because of his family the university had represented him in court and the sentence was commuted to two days in the stocks, where he had to absorb the scorn and taunts of all the youngsters.

If anything, the punishment had made him worse. He was not a gifted scholar, and had already disgraced the town for five long years. He was big in the shoulders and hips, and was given to almost constant brawling. Despite a scar from a saber in some long-forgotten duel, his face appeared boyish and innocent. With a mop of light hair falling over the forehead and with cheeks that were gaunt, at a quick glance he did not look unlike Tilman von Rothenau.

How many dozen students he had in tow Ingi could not count. She did know he was up to some devilment, perhaps stealing flour from the mill and daubing up the Ratshaus. Only when his voice was close enough to understand did she tremble for herself.

"There she is," he taunted, "that sorceress—that bastard child of a witch and the devil!" His voice was

"There she is," he taunted.

heavy, like a clap of rolling thunder, and he had had
enough wine to make him more than a little wobbly.
He stood directly before the stall, not two paces away,
hurling epithets. A tear rolled down Ingi's cheek, but
in a mixture of fear and anger she balled her fist and
struck out at him.

"Get her, boys, rush her!" Turk grabbed her fists and
wrestled her hard to the cobblestones. Against the bull-
like muscles she squirmed and screamed, but it was like

fighting bars of iron. She struck out with her sandals and caught him square in the stomach. For a second he was winded.

A dozen students scrambled over the stall and pinned her to the pavement. Catching his breath again, Turk grasped her wrists in one huge fist and sat firmly on her chest, while a companion immobilized her flailing feet. "That's it, Hunk. Now, Pete! Give it the old heave-ho."

The students hoisted her trays over their heads, took five or six running steps, and dashed them into the stream. "Stop it, stop it!" the girl screamed. "Call the guards. Help! Help!"

The housewives who crowded the pavement simply kept their distance and looked on, as if in truth they hardly considered themselves capable of stopping a score of drunken students. Everything splashed into the Faule Bach—the hazelnuts, the carrots, the cabbages, the turnips, the beets, the honey, the crate of chickens. Last of all, with Ingi still screeching for help and the boys warming to the excitement, three of them crouched behind the cart, worked up a head of steam, and sent it careening over the curb and into the water.

Ingi was frantic. The cart alone was worth as much as she could earn in a month, and her wares were the only thing of value to keep her family warm and clothed through the winter. But no valiant hero came to the rescue. With her wrists still tightly locked in his grip, Turk struggled to his feet. While his companion grabbed her by the ankles and he by the wrists, they half carried, half dragged her over the stones, swung her twice over the curbing and dropped her into the ditch.

She hit hard against the surface, like a tossed cat fighting to land on all fours. The icy water took her breath away. The momentum carried her completely under, though the stream was scarcely three feet deep. After a second or two she found her footing and struggled dripping to the wall. Around her floated the debris of her stall. Fortunately, the water had cushioned her fall, although she probably would be black and blue.

The top of the curbing rose level with her eyes. As she tried to climb out, the whole market place took on the appearance of a battlefield. Cart after cart was being shoved into the Faule Bach, except for those that provided good ammunition.

The air quivered with beets and turnips, and a continuing tinkle of glass sounded from the town hall and the shops around the square. Two score students formed a line of battle before the great doors of the Ratshaus, firing a hail of vegetables at the outraged shopkeepers and housewives.

In the chill air Ingi shivered. Her hair hung loose and wet, and her rose cap went floating down toward the mill. She tried to boost herself out, but without much success. Everyone else was launching turnips, ducking them, or nursing a bruise. No one had time to help a market girl.

With one foot on a protruding brick, she pushed her way up the wall. A pair of strong hands caught her beneath the arms and lifted her from the stream. Grateful but surprised, she took a step backward and nearly fell in again. Her benefactor wore the cape of a student, and the mischievous grin on his face showed he was not above enjoying how ungainly she looked.

"You do look a bit like a witch," he chuckled. "*Now,* at least. That's what started it all wasn't it? Not that I believe in witches, mind you. Not in the Year of Our Lord 1520. My grandfather, yes. But nobody believes in witches now. That was just an excuse."

At his infectious grin Ingi smiled, but she was still reserved. It was not that her dignity bothered her; it was the loss of all those wares and the cart. The chickens she might still save. "I guess I really ought to thank you, though you can imagine what I think of students."

"At your service, Fräulein. We aren't all destructive. If you need help, just call for Eberhard Bostler, law student from Nürnberg."

Heavy boots sounded on the Schlossgasse, and horsemen galloped from the Jüdenquartier. The men quickly cut off the exits of the square, unsheathing swords and flashing halberds in the sunlight. The *Unteroffizier* shouted a command and they dashed in phalanx against the embattled students, then halted two yards short of running them through. The shriek of the melee faded to silence. At one sight of naked steel the students paled. They were no longer ferocious wolves but cowed boys. In another minute the guard encircled their quarry and marched them off to the garrison.

Even with the sun warm on her face Ingi shivered. "As long as I'm wet anyway," she said laughing, "maybe I should haul out the chickens and see if I can salvage the cart."

Eberhard liked the clean sweep of her upturned nose and the sparkle of her chatter. "If you'll wait till I take off my boots and doublet, I'll give you a hand." Two minutes later they were both splashing in the stream as playfully as ducklings.

CHAPTER EIGHT

THE HERETIC LUTHER

Just before dusk on a drizzly September day Tilman von Rothenau pulled his cap tight about his ears and his cape snug about his throat. The droplets of water were tiny, driven hard by the wind until they seemed to pierce even the skin.

The Collegiengasse stood empty, with damp leaves skittering across the cobblestones. Tilman glanced up just in time to avoid a student scampering home to the bursa.

The wrought-iron gates of the Augustinian Cloister stood open. In the whole courtyard they were the only attraction that caught the eye. An old wooden fence that once cut off the monastery from the town had long ago fallen into disrepair, with missing boards and cracks and knots showing the damage of too many snows. Even the courtyard was the worse for wear, with broken paving-stones and the still unraked pear leaves. A border of flowers near the gate stood brown and gaunt, killed by a hard frost, and the only spot of living green was a patch of myrtle under a tree.

Off to the left a tiny wooden chapel, haphazardly milled and carpentered, was lit with the flicker of candle-light. Despite the howl of the wind Tilman could make out the chanting of the monks. In the main building straight ahead an occasional light glimmered where lay brothers were preparing the evening meal.

Tilman had expected to find a student or two still hanging about the classrooms, but the ill weather had sent them all home to their pensions or dormitories. A lone cook appeared at the door of the kitchen, wrapped about the waist with a towel, and flung a pot of steaming water out across the cobblestones.

Tilman hurried. "Tell me, please, where would I find Doctor Luther? They've sent me from the Klein print shop."

"It's far too late, apprentice. Vespers is nearly done, and though he might be kind enough to see you after he's through preaching and eating, you shouldn't really disturb him. Why not come back in the morning, after matins?" The door swung shut to all but a crack, keeping out the wind.

Tilman grinned at the efficient little cook. "But he sent word to come fetch a manuscript. Not an hour ago. If we start composing at daylight, we can save two hours."

"All right, if you're so persistent." The cook opened the door and came out into the wind. "Come with me."

They walked to the end of the three-story building and picked their way up a treacherously narrow staircase, in the full blast of the wind. At the second floor they turned off through a roofed walkway, open to the air but cut off from the rain. "That's the prior's room there. I'll tell him you're waiting. But mind, don't waste his time. We don't want him missing supper."

Even before Tilman could reply the man in the apron limped swiftly away. In the lee of the building the air was comparatively warm and dry. Tilman sought out a bench, pulled his cape tight about the neck, and peered out over the courtyard, with elbows on the rail. Across the way in the tiny chapel he saw the candles flicker and move. In the last glimmer of daylight the black-robed monks filed quietly from their vespers and marched to the refectory.

The last to leave, clutching a scrap of sermon notes in his hand, was the prior. In the darkness Tilman could get only a vague impression—that he was husky and broad-shouldered but did not have the carriage of an athlete; that he moved quickly despite his size; that there was purpose in his stride.

He did not march in step with his fellow Augustinians —there could have been scarcely twenty—but strode against the wind, his black robes flying, toward the open stairwell. The man in the apron met him at the landing, whispered a few words, and then disappeared. Luther mounted the steps two at a time.

"There you are, apprentice! You're the boy from Master Melchior's?"

"Yes, sir."

"Thank you for coming so quickly. Wolf tells me to make you wait until I've had my supper, but that would scarcely be Christian, would it? Besides, you would miss yours. I wish I could take you to the refectorium. But we monks are supposed to eat in silence. If the others can't have guests, neither should the prior. Tell me, what's your name?"

"Tilman, Herr Doctor. Tilman von Rothenau."

"Oh, yes. I've heard the name. Your father was a squire, wasn't he? Torgau, I think."

"How did you know, sir?"

"Well, I've lived all over Saxony, at one time or another. And with students from all over, one does pick up odd bits and names." The monk swung his robes back out of the way and pushed open the door of his study. "Excuse me for going first. I'll make a light so you don't stumble over the desk or chairs."

In the glimmer of a pair of candles Tilman got his first good look at Martin Luther. The monk appeared younger than he had expected, still in his mid-thirties, but there was a look of maturity and understanding in his face, far beyond what one would expect in a man so young. He twiddled with the silver cross that hung from his cincture.

"I've heard good things of you, Tilman. From Master Lucas."

"Thank you, sir."

"I wish we could keep you here in Wittenberg. He tells me you're keen on printing and want to learn the trade in Mainz. Mainz has its masters—don't let me belittle them. So have Paris and Basel and Venice. But we're not far behind, and there's more printing to be done in Wittenberg than in all of them. God's printing."

Tilman could not find words to say what was really in his heart: that the religious climate in Wittenberg bothered him far more than he cared to say, and that Luther was largely responsible.

The prior rummaged through the papers atop his desk. Off in the corner a stove of Bavarian tiles shed warmth and a soft glow of light, and a mongrel puppy stirred from his sleep at the sound of voices. At the far window the wind pushed the rain hard against the leaded glass, with just a trace of daylight still on the horizon.

"Master Melchior, as you know, is one of the best printers in town. For one thing, he has the finest fonts. Clean, new, well-designed, easy to read. Much of my printing goes off to the other masters (Gruenenberg, Rhau, Weiss, and Lotther) although of course there's too much for any one of them. If only I could compose directly in type and save you those weary hours over a chase!" There was a mischievous smile on his features.

"No, sir—we'd lose our jobs. You stick to preaching and we'll do the printing."

The monk guffawed. "The elector was so pleased with the job on the *German Nobility* that Master Melchior deserves more manuscripts. It's not just that God's truth cries out for printing. It demands *good* printing. And Master Melchior certainly deserves a share of my manuscripts." He paused a moment. "Easy there, Toelpel. He's just a printer's boy. You're supposed to growl only at papal nuncios." Tilman was not completely certain the comment was amusing, but he had to admit it was forthright and honest, if nothing else. Luther may have been plain-spoken but he was certainly no deceiver.

"I won't keep you, sir. The man in the apron said you were about to eat."

"What's another meal more or less, when a man has

grown up fasting? Still, let me get you the manuscripts."
He shuffled through the loose papers on an old oak
table. The wooden surface bore stains of ink, and on the
legs the worms had had a picnic boring through the
fibers.

"Here they are. Three short manuscripts. I've already
described them to Master Melchior, and he'll know
what to expect. That's the postil, there. The one for
the duke. Just a little homily on faith and the Scriptures
I did for His Grace while he was so sick this summer.
And something on the creed—*The Short Form of the
Creed* I've called it—for family use. And a Sendtbrief
on usury the lawyers in Leipzig wanted."

He held out the little sheaf of papers toward Tilman, quickly changed his mind, and put them back on
the desk. With supple fingers he rolled them into a
sheet of brown paper and tied them with a string. "My
writing is too hard to read even without rainspots.
Maybe a bit of wrapping would prove a big blessing
to the typesetters."

"Yes, sir. I'll carry it inside my cape, and it'll stay
dry." Tilman rose to leave.

"Stay a minute, if you like. You haven't even met my
dog." The monk stepped thoughtfully to the window,
warming his hands before the tiles of the stove. He sat
down on the leather pad of the bench, appearing totally
relaxed, with the raindrops drumming on the window.

"You look worried, lad, more so than a boy your age ought. And don't argue. I've seen plenty of men your age—novices, students, by the thousand. What's bothering you? Something at the print shop? Being cooped up in Wittenberg, with Mainz too far away?"

The question caught Tilman unawares. "It's the family Tannenlohe, Herr Professor. They always seem to need me. First the mother is ducked in the millpond, and then the daughter in the Faule Bach. It's not that I have any real obligation; it's just that I hate to leave them unprotected."

"The Tannenlohes, eh? You should have known the father. An ox of a man, but one who worked hard and wisely for his brood. A woodcutter and charcoal burner, until a beech fell the wrong way and crushed his ribs. We used to know him well at the cloister, for he supplied our firewood."

"You know them? Maybe you could explain something, sir, if you have a moment. Why is it the villagers are so set on harming them? What little I've seen, the widow Tannenlohe is no more a witch than I. A kindly, hard-working woman who spends long hours to keep the youngsters clothed and fed. But the Kronbergers despise the ground she treads on."

"You're too much of a city boy, Tilman. That's the way life is in the village. I suppose you've also heard about Frater Heidrich? I really shouldn't say this—it might be a sin against the Eighth Commandment. But he's too far away from his superiors, and there's not much doubt he's switched his allegiance from Jehovah to Beelzebub, or whoever the lord of greed may be. If the widow dies, witch or not, the property goes to the parish; in this case, to the Dominicans. But don't fret. The town fathers know all about it, and the good brother will get his comeuppance."

Now that his eyes had grown used to the dim light, Tilman examined the far crannies of the room. Overhead, the beams divided the large room into squares, with frescoes from the Scriptures worked into the plaster. Behind the desk stood a priedieu, and on the wall above it, a brass crucifix. At the window ledge a tiny marble statue of the Madonna looked out over the floodlands of the Elbe. The walls bore paintings and etchings one might expect in an abbot's quarters—a map of German territories and Augustinian chapter houses, a painting of the monk's parents, and a portrait of St. Jerome poring over the Vulgate.

"It's good to hear you say so, Father. I worry about the Tannenlohes. Not just them, but others like them. With no champion, with no food or breadwinner, and with no money even to pay the taxes, they wind up either in the poorhouse or the grave. There's no other choice."

"Things change, Tilman. Fifty years ago your father

"Tell me, how would you describe God?"

doubtless felt the same way, and look at the improvements! As long as the good Lord's up there, we're in good hands."

"I hope you're right, Herr Doktor. Sometimes it looks hopeless."

"Tell me, apprentice, how would you describe God? As a kindly old grandfather who treats his children with affection? As a hard-hearted slave-master who scourges without mercy? As a usurious money-lender who tries to sell you a ticket to paradise in exchange for good works? Or is he a gracious king who gives it to you generously, without a price?"

The question was so sudden and so intense that Tilman stared dully at the pattern of light flickering from the door of the stove. Outside he could hear the bells of the Stadtkirche tolling the curfew, even over the noise of the wind. His face suddenly brightened.

"I see what you mean, sir, even if my years are few. Now that we've a chance to read the Scriptures—not many of us, mind you, but three times as many as in my grandfather's day—we have a clearer picture of God, through the Jesus who stood by the Samarian well, the Jesus who healed lepers, the Jesus who forgave Simon. He is not just a stern old Jehovah who sat on Mt. Sinai and thundered commandments. Not a God who only demands, but one who also gives."

"Exactly. I couldn't have phrased it better."

"If this is what you teach, sir, why have you so many enemies? The bishops and archbishops, the nuncios and chamberlains, and if rumor is right, even the Holy Father?"

"Sometimes the truth is obscured. People like to think they are paying their own way, even to heaven. The church has encouraged them in this belief for too long. Even if the church does approve, it's wrong. Seeking heaven through good works hides the whole purpose of Christ's suffering and death."

"Excuse me for seeming to argue, reverend sir. I was taught by my mother to kneel, and if there was any doubt between kneeling and thinking, to kneel."

"Your mother must have been a wise woman. Christ said something like that when he suggested we must be like little children if we are to enter the kingdom of heaven."

In ordinary circumstances Tilman might not have been so forward, but his companion gave him every encouragement. He felt at ease in the abbot's study.

"Tell me, sir, if I may be so bold, why is it that you who are a monk oppose monasteries? And how can you celebrate the holy office day after day, if you do not believe the bread changes into Christ's body? And how can you call the Holy Father a man of God and yet question the whole system of bishoprics and papacy?"

Luther's eyes flickered with laughter. "It's obvious we're not going to get any supper tonight," he said. He took out a sack of chestnuts from his desk and put them on a tin plate, which he slid under the grate. "The Brothers of the Common Life must have taught you well. They were my teachers, too, at Magdeburg. To ask such penetrating questions shows that your eyes and ears have been wide open. How long have you been in Wittenberg?"

"Seven weeks, sir."

"Ah. Not long at all. And you should be about ready for the trip to Mainz?"

"Yes, Father."

"Then I'd better talk to you. I've written a score of books and pamphlets on those questions, lectured on them, preached about them. I'd hate to have a native Saxon leave us for the Rhineland with the wrong idea of what that heretic Luther really teaches."

The prior's mood was so jovial and at the same time so serious that Tilman hung on his words as if they were a magnet. The chestnuts were steaming now, with an occasional pop followed by a little yelp from Toelpel. Luther raked out a handful of nuts from the ashes where they lay cooling on the wooden parquetry.

"Let's start with the Lord's Supper, Tilman. That's as sacred a subject as you can find; how God can be present in the bread and wine, and how the human mind can accept this. Perhaps the whole idea is like the wood in the fire there. Wood can change its form and appearance. It is no longer hard and brown and cold. Now it glows with heat and light. But it is still wood."

"Then you do not really believe that the bread changes into the body?"

"Not completely. I can't find it in the Word of God. That's the reason I doubt it. God *is* present. So much Paul assures us. Just how—ah, there's the mystery. As the Latin puts it, *in, with,* and *through* the eating. But I wouldn't want to stake my faith that bread was no longer bread, or that only the priest was good enough for the wine. That smacks to me of man, and not of God."

Tilman was not altogether happy about this explanation. From his toddling days he had been taught to revere the host as the body of Christ. When a golden monstrance was paraded through the streets on Corpus Christi Day he was as willing to pay homage to it as to the Savior himself.

The monk probed a nut with his fingers, then peeled the steaming husk from it. He offered the meat to the dog, who gulped it down greedily. The second he shared with his fair-haired guest.

"I can't ask you to accept what I teach. I cannot even ask this of my monks or my students. But I do ask that you give me a hearing. The devil has won more battles because the enemy fled in terror than through armed conflict. Good, clear thinking, based on the Word, never hurt anybody. It's those who always accept at face value anything the church suggests who are apt to fall off the tightrope. Now, then, I've gotten so excited I forgot what else you asked about."

Tilman pulled at the lobe of his ear, a habit his mother used to scold him about. His boyish blue eyes showed his youthful concern, and yet he was enjoying the conversation. He rolled the manuscripts more tightly between his fingers.

"The office of the papacy, Dr. Martin, and the question of the monasteries."

"Ah, yes. They're not easy, son, any of your questions. When does a dutiful and obedient son of a squire, like you, become disloyal and disobedient? The borderline is not at all clear. My point is this. The papacy (I'm not singling out Leo) has fallen into the hands of the money-changers and has ceased to be the office of the servant of the servants of God. The pope buys and sells palliums to the highest bidder. He forgives sins—for a price. In the hands of the Medici even the papacy can be bartered. Things are so out of hand that we have had three different popes at the same time, each claiming the divine right."

The rain had slackened on the window now, but the wind blew with increasing fury. "And what of the monks, Father?"

"The monks? There are just too many of us. One of every four men in Germany. Franciscans, Dominicans, Augustinians, Carmelites. We pray, we beg, we say the offices. But we don't teach the common folk and we don't read the Gospel. We build costly monasteries. We take a vow of poverty, yet scheme to steal from widows. We take a vow of chastity, yet openly father children. We take a vow of obedience—here I'm at fault

—yet question whether the vow was really to God or only to our superiors."

In the flicker of the candles Luther had grown less light-hearted. His face appeared sober, almost too sober. With a conscious effort he tried to break the spell by offering more chestnuts. "You see, Tilman, we all have our problems. You: your future, learning a trade, your vow to your mother, your sympathy toward the Tannen-lohes. Me: my monastic oath, my trust in the Lord, my reading of Scriptures, my differences with the Roman curia, my obligations to my parents, and even more, to the scores of students I influence every day. God does not make life easy, does he, Tilman?"

Suddenly the prior appeared in the role of a kindly grandfather, not an energetic teacher in his mid-thirties. For a few minutes they stared in silence out through the leaded windows. Forty paces away the town crier was making his rounds along the ramparts of the wall. His voice drifted faintly over the monastery walls, "Nine o'clock, and all's well."

Tilman had grown as contemplative as the monk. His eyes appeared troubled, and there was a set to his face that brought furrows to his brow. He put the manu-script under his arm and grasped at the cloak crumpled on the bench beside him. Luther followed him to the door, with a lighted candlestick in his hand. In parting he made the sign of the cross.

"And with thy spirit," Tilman responded, from the ritual of the mass.

Tilman swung open the door to the timbered gangway, a walking place for the monks. Luther's face danced with shadows caused by the candle. "Tell me, Tilman. If *you* were the Holy Father, would *you* call me a heretic?"

Tilman wished the question had not been asked. The cold air bit into his face, after the warmth of the study. He pulled his cap tight. "I don't know, Dr. Luther. I honestly don't know. Perhaps only God can say."

"We leave it in his hands then?" The monk was once more serious. "Go in peace, lad."

"Thank you, Father." Tilman's boots echoed on the fir planks of the gangway. The crack of light from the door vanished. Leaning into the wind, he turned the corner into the Collegiengasse. He had forgotten to thank the monk for his hospitality. But tonight his heart spilled over with greater things than social graces.

CHAPTER NINE

THE COUNCIL'S DEBATE

The dozen burghers sitting around the table might have stepped directly from a painting of Albrecht Dürer. Each had made his mark, in his own way, and each had been honored with the title of councilman. In a free city like Wittenberg this was scarcely below the title of duke or even king. The twelve lounged around the table with a kind of mock importance—successful and, for the most part, well-to-do.

The council chambers would have done honor to a far larger city than Wittenberg. The Rathaus itself was more than two hundred years old, and though its beams were beginning to sag, it still boasted an honorable and rugged splendor. Except for the chambers of the elector it was doubtless the best-appointed building in town.

115

Around the walls ranged life-size portraits of each of the councilmen, done in somber colors. Each wore the most formal attire, with the gold chain of office around the neck. The floor boasted a Bruges carpet of softest wool, and on the far wall where there were no windows the ancient plaster was covered by an old but still majestic tapestry. It depicted a stag hunt, with the beaters and dogs working through a bog, while the mounted hunting party waited on solid land.

At what might be considered the head of the huge round-table, Bürgermeister Hans Memel struck a mood of disinterested interest. He recognized the prestige of his position; in terms of authority he was as important as the duke. However, he was a successful goldsmith, and sometimes gave the impression he might prefer to be in his workshop, among his punches and molds and apprentices, rather than wasting a morning a week of his valuable time at the Town Hall.

The table over which he presided was even more pretentious than the council chamber. A magnificent old piece of furniture, it could hardly have been the work of an ordinary provincial cabinetmaker—that huge block of cherry so neatly selected and fitted one could scarcely find the joints, and so large the cleaning woman needed a long-handled feather duster to reach the middle. The chairs, of fine grain and rich, red finish, matched the table and had scarlet velour on the seats and backs.

There were fifteen or eighteen, doubtless the most cherished furnishings of the council chambers.

"Councilmen"—the Bürgermeister rapped on the table—"I fear we shall not finish if we don't tend strictly to business. I am well aware that some of these problems may seem inconsequential, but if they are legally presented and if they are items which might have wider import, we have no choice but to hear them." He looked about him at eleven disinterested faces. "You have heard the report of the comptroller. What disposition do you suggest in the matter of the lantern boy?"

There was at first no response. Finally Erding Helmut pursed his lips, speaking in the thin voice of a tired old man. "With all due respect, Herr Bürgermeister, if we can no longer continue to hire a lantern boy to go before the Bürgermeister for a groschen per evening, considering the candles cost an additional groschen per hour, I recommend Your Lordship dispense with the lantern boy altogether. Our poor treasury cannot stand frivolity."

There was a ripple of amusement around the table. The Bürgermeister frowned and coughed self-consciously. "That will be enough, Herr Councilman. It is not me we are thinking of—it is the dignity of the office. I will inquire further to find another boy at the old rate, and if I am still unsuccessful, perhaps I can persuade one of my wife's nephews."

Halfway around the table Lucas Cranach stroked the waxed mustache that lay curled between lip and chin, like the curved horns of a ram. In velvet doublet and hose, with a chestnut-colored shoulderstrap to anchor the gold-hilted sword, he looked the model of a wealthy and important burgher.

"Mein Herr," said Cranach, "with your persuasive ability I am sure you will be able to solve the difficulty of the lantern boy. But one item of business I think is extremely important. Last week we commissioned the legal counselor to make a full investigation of the market rioting. I see several sheets of paper before Herr Stadtrat Worden, and I know all of us are eager for his report."

The lawyer glanced respectfully toward the Bürgermeister and got a nod in return. He cleared his throat. "Gentlemen, I am most pleased to serve you. It's been a busy week, with three appearances in court, plus all the developments from the riot. But the whole intrigue has been uncovered, and of course it demands your attention and action."

There were murmurs of "On with it," and "Get down to business," though as usual the young and conceited lawyer appeared to ignore the complaints.

"I have talked to more than a score of students. The university authorities have been helpful, even when they had to withdraw one or another of the students from a lecture." His voice had a touch of honey, as if he were trying to influence a judge or witness. "As some of you may have guessed, the real culprit was Turk Stutzer, the medical student from Frankfurt. You may also recall he had difficulties last spring and was put on probation by the university."

The Bürgermeister harrumphed, as if the story was growing too lengthy. The lawyer paid no heed. His pace and voice did not change.

"Turk has not returned to the bursa since the day of the riot. Obviously he intended to embarrass only the Tannenlohe girl, but the fun-making got out of hand, with all the wine. The university dismissed him immediately and there are reports that he is roaming the countryside, seeking work as a field hand, though at this time of the year there is little work. He comes of common parents—there is almost no money we could recover for the damages."

"Then what do you recommend? Shall we order a warrant for his arrest?"

The lawyer resented the intrusion. "There is much more to the story, my lord counselors. One of the students told me of plotting the night before at the Gasthof Golden Eagle, on the road to Coswig. The innkeeper would perhaps not have been so talkative, had the students not broken his best flagon. Frater Heidrich was also there. The innkeeper swears the Dominican plotted the whole raid, to get his hands on the inheritance. The monk paid for the beer. The eight students who were there he gave ten groschen apiece—enough to keep them drunk for a week."

Cranach interrupted. "Herr Stadtrat, have you solid evidence that Heidrich was the instigator? Or was this just the word of the innkeeper?"

"I have, sir. After I talked to the taverner I questioned the students again. Two admitted they had been paid to dump the girl's wares into the millrace. The monk has not slept in his quarters for a week, not since the day of the riot."

"Then he suspects his secret is out?" The questioner was Lothar Hartig, a dealer in costly cloth who always dressed in the best stuffs his shop could provide. By now the whole council had snapped out of its lackadaisical attitude and sat alert and intent.

"He must. No doubt he's sorry he gave the conspirators so much beer money. That turned what began as a practical joke into a riot (a riot, I might add, that he may not have planned). Now he will lose everything, probably even his cassock."

The issue grew more heated by the minute. Reiner Tölke, the owner of a bakeshop, leaped to his feet as quickly as if the loaves in his ovens were going up in smoke. "Can't we throw all the monks out of town—all but the Augustinians? God knows they contribute nothing to our town, begging for their food and stirring up the peasants and sucking the blood of the workers."

The Bürgermeister rapped for order. The issue was an exciting one, no longer just a question of Frau Pollack complaining about the hay her neighbor's horses trod into the earth, or the color of tile for the public baths, or a disease among the geese that spoiled the eggs.

"This is not a matter completely within our jurisdiction, gentlemen," said the Bürgermeister. "We are charged with the peace and order of the town. To that extent we have full authority to investigate the riot. Frater Heidrich, however, is subject only to Canon Law. Meister Lucas was on the right track. All we can do is make a complete and impartial report of our investigations to the superior of the Dominican order. We may have to go all the way to the vicar general. In the meanwhile I suggest we curb our passions. The church courts take time, I admit, but in the end their sentences are as severe as those of the civil courts."

"What you say is correct," Reinhard Zillerthal interrupted. "Yet if we are to be the leaders of this free city and to carry out its work as the elector expects, we cannot close our eyes to wrong or injustice simply because it originates with the clergy. I suggest that we support those efforts of the church which encourage the best interests of the citizenry. For example, if Professor

Luther should be summoned to a council, as all the rumors suggest, I feel that we should pay his travel expenses, and if necessary, hire a carriage wherever he might be required to go: Heidelberg, Leipzig, Frankfurt, Cologne."

The conversation had swung so quickly from the devilry of Frater Heidrich to the daring position of Luther that the chambers buzzed. Zillerthal grinned impishly at his coup. The Bürgermeister knew it was impossible to restore order, and he took his mug of cider, flavored with a touch of raspberry juice, and stood beside the open window.

The sash was flung wide to the air, on as beautiful and sunny a day of St. Martin's summer as one could imagine. In the square below, an occasional passerby lolled under the half-leafless branches of the lindens or lingered in the doorway of a shop.

Standing near the window His Worship, Hans Memel the Bürgermeister, raised his voice to a pitch not ordinarily reached by a goldsmith who spent most of his hours poring over an engraving tool or casting a delicate mold or setting a pearl.

"The policy of the council," he said, "is to remain scrupulously impartial in matters which do not directly affect our realm of activity. Even the duke himself chooses such a course. If Luther is right, if monasticism is a thing of evil and the writs of indulgence do destroy

"The policy of this council is to remain impartial."

faith, then Luther will conquer without our help. If he is wrong and if the church wishes to burn him at the stake, as it did Hus, the council should be the first to support the decision of the courts. We have no authority to encourage him, any more than we have the right to discourage him."

At this declaration of neutrality there was a renewed outburst among the councilmen, on the one hand by those who, like the Bürgermeister, desired a hands-off policy, and by those who wished instead to give Luther their support. The banging of pewter mugs on the old table gradually quieted. Cranach quietly but decisively pushed back his chair and took the floor.

"As for me, Herr Bürgermeister, this is not a private issue between Luther and Mother Church. Perhaps you are right in saying the council should not become involved. But this certainly does not mean we as individuals should not become involved. The matter of my salvation—or yours, or that of your grandchildren—is not merely the concern of the church. God expects every leader to take a stand, and to use his leadership to support what he considers right."

There was a wave of applause and a stamping of feet when Cranach sat down, but also a restrained murmur from those who sided with the Bürgermeister.

From one of the clerk's offices down the hall a waiter entered with a pitcher of cider. "That will do, Herr Ober," the goldsmith shouted, waving the newcomer away with a sweep of the hand. "Will you please leave the pitcher and go."

He turned back toward the councilmen. "Gentlemen, our hearts are too inflamed to talk intelligently. I hereby adjourn the session. We will return promptly in half an hour and be in our seats when the clock in the Stadtkirche strikes eleven. The name of Luther will not be mentioned. At that time we will discuss the final wording of our recommendation to the Dominican superior concerning Heidrich. Herr Zillerthal and the Herr Stadtrat will now formulate a draft. Gentlemen, you are dismissed."

By ones and twos the burghers dawdled from the room, down the stairway, past the public scales and the Ratskeller, to quiet their emotions in the mellow October sun.

CHAPTER TEN

THE MILLS OF GOD

Like many a hard-working burgher, Melchior Klein hated holy days. He did not mind stopping his press and putting aside the tympan for Good Friday or Christmas or Epiphany or even St. John's Day. But the scores of minor festivals like Candlemas and St. Martin's and Corpus Christi and St. Sebastian's continually annoyed him.

He knew better than to operate his press on a day the church proclaimed holy, for its clanking would disturb the whole neighborhood. Every clergyman in town would hound him. He also knew better than to ask his apprentices to work, or to call in the journeymen. The law of the land was strict, and even for the first offense he would probably be given a fine of at least

two gulden. Melchior had a great amount of printing
almost continually piled on his work table and he hated
to give up forty or more working days every year, in
addition to Sundays. There was scarcely a week when
there was not a holiday, and some weeks had two or
three.

On the morning of St. Michael's and All Angels,
with the journeymen either at home or at church, Melchior hunched over the composing desk and set type
for a new treatise by Philip Melanchthon. It was not
that Melchior disliked the church or considered himself
a bad Catholic, but he thought one mass a week was
enough. A look of guilt on his face betrayed his feelings, although with the door of the workshop locked
from the inside and without the noise of the press, no
one could prove he was breaking the sabbath. He consoled himself as he set up paragraph after paragraph
of the book of postils. This was as solidly religious as
anything he would hear in church, and besides, he felt
he had a pressing obligation to get it into print as soon
as possible. To justify himself further he tried to recall
what he had once heard Luther say about the monastic
offices: that one could be just as good a monk by going
to chapel once a day, out of sincerity, as a dozen times,
out of habit. By going to church a man did not auto-
matically fling open the gates of paradise; only God
could do that.

Though Tilman had not said a word about the holy day and surely had heard the summons of the Stadt-kirche bells, he sat beside his master. He had entered only a step behind Melchior, before the door was locked, and the master said nothing and pretended not to notice. Melchior had no fears he would be betrayed; Tilman was as guilty as he.

In their six weeks together the status of the new apprentice really had not been clarified. Tilman still talked enthusiastically of the trip to Mainz. Melchior expressed his regret at losing so good a workman, but realized he had no claim on the lad.

There was no legal agreement about the apprentice-ship, with a formal exchange of papers and oaths involving master, apprentice, and guildmeister, as was usually the case. Of course, in the field of printing, even what used to be customary was getting to be an exception because of the blossoming trade. Melchior had no actual agreement at all with Tilman, except that the boy would do what he could, that Melchior would feed and teach him, and supply a few groschen a week for spending money. The payments an apprentice's parents sometimes made were in this case generously paid by Lucas, in thanks for what Tilman had done for Hans.

If Melchior had had a normal conscience about money, he might have felt guilty about the arrangement. Tilman already knew so much of the trade that he ought to be getting the salary of a journeyman. Melchior salved his conscience only because the terms were so short, Tilman was so young, and Lucas had money to burn.

Melchior was pleased to see Tilman on the stool beside him, with the font of type. It showed that Tilman liked him, even if it meant working on a holiday.

Immediately after lunch Tilman threaded his way out of the Scharrengasse behind the Rathaus to the town mill. Ever since the day he had met Reinhard Zillerthal at the village of Kronberg he had wanted to get to know him. Obviously, the beak-nosed old bachelor had meant his invitation sincerely.

Unlike the tiny waterwheels out in the countryside, the town mill was one of Wittenberg's most imposing structures. Beside the massive castle and the Schlosskirche its bulk did not appear so imposing as it really was, or as it would have been among the thatched cottages of the Jewish Quarter or the Elster Quarter, where there were gardens and pastureland.

For nearly a block the Rische Bach and the Faule Bach raced side by side, not fifty feet apart. The stone paving of the millraces gave the water considerable momentum as it raced toward the mill wheels. A narrow cutoff and two sluices allowed either stream to power either wheel.

On the feast day of St. Michael the Archangel both wheels were quiet, and the water sluiced noisily along, bypassing the mill and dashing harmlessly under the

Coswigerstrasse and out through the town wall. Wisps of smoke drifted from a chimney high overhead, and for this reason Tilman assumed his host was at home.

He climbed an open stairway just inside the walls. The building was high, long, and narrow, built to accommodate the mill and yet give ample room for the highway and the castle. The first two floors were filled with the bulky machinery of the mill: the wheels with their cupped blades, the wooden gearing and tackle and blocks, the two pairs of millstones broader than a man's reach, the chutes for loading grain and sacking flour, cranes and pulleys for unloading the wagons.

As Tilman worked his way up the stairs, poorly lighted on such an overcast day, the lean, ruddy face of Reinhard Zillerthal poked round the corner. "There you are, laddie. I was beginning to think you'd classed me as a witch-hunter or journeyed on toward Mainz. Glad to see you're still wi' us."

By its size the room must once have been a vast granary. Long before Reinhard's day, perhaps back in his grandfather's, the whole floor had been converted to living quarters. The ceilings were high, and there was a touch of flour about the window sills, but it was comfortably furnished with leather chairs and a bed built into an alcove.

For a bachelor like Reinhard it offered room to spare. About the walls on pegs in the masonry stood a display of crossbows and arquebuses and even matchlocks. The miller's quick eyes noted Tilman's interest. "The Lord spare me from boasting, but it's the best sporting armory in Wittenberg, barring the duke's."

"How did a miller ever get so interested in shooting?"

"Well, laddie, it's that I'm not really a miller; I guess that explains it. But it's a good income, being a miller, and all I have to do is keep the records—the others do the work. It's a rather lazy way to live, I suppose, but can I help it if my grandfather and the old duke hit it off so well? And if I hadn't inherited the job as royal miller, I wouldn't be a hunter, either, but just a common poacher. If the duke's guards caught me with a haunch of venison, I'd wind up in chains. This way it's perfectly respectable."

Tilman took a crossbow from the wall. He had seen such weapons often as a boy, but only the rougher sort used by a soldier. This one was hand-crafted, a work of art. The steel of the bow appeared to be of Damascus, with a stag inlaid in silver on one side and a hunter on the other. The trigger-catch was filed bright as a mirror, and the bowstring was new and well oiled.

Reinhard extended his arms with the palms up. "Come snowfall, perhaps you'd like to try it for rabbits. I'm allowed to share the hunting rights—for small game, at least. Not for stags, but grouse and rabbits. As you see," he pointed to the loden jacket over his arm and a leather vest still unbuttoned, "I was about to head for the Karpfenteich. On so overcast a day, the eels and perch get hungry. Only the carp stay near the bottom. Come along?"

Tilman was so intrigued by the intricate workmanship of the crossbow that he was not listening as attentively as he might. A little startled, he replied, "Oh, yes. I'd love to."

Leaving the mounted antlers and the display of weapons, they went down the back stairs. "It's rather a damp home for steel, over the millrace. My falcons don't like it, either. I keep them in cages in the loft, near the dormers. At that height they can see far out over the valley. Not that it does them much good. I don't use them much. Falconing is best when it's warm, and of course that's when the game is poorest. But I will say this. Except for the watchman on the Marienkirche, they have the best view in town."

With a bag of fishing gear over his shoulder and a pair of rods in his hand the miller led his young companion out into the Coswigerstrasse. The sky overhead was darkened by low-hanging blankets of clouds, which made it look as if there might be snow in the air, but the warm mist hinted more of fog than of snow.

They decided to walk through the town rather than along the banks of the moat. From the fall rains the waters were high, and there was no telling if they could manage the soggy footing in the meadows.

The town square was nearly empty, as if all the burghers were sleeping the afternoon away or had departed on picnics. Once past the dormitories and the Augustinian Cloister, they came to open land. Next came the Elstertor, with its cannon emplacements and drawbridge.

A quick swing to the north, perhaps a ten-minute walk, brought them to the duke's fish pond. "It's amusing, you know," the miller confided. "I'd probably catch just as many eels if I let down a net in the millrace. My mother always did. It's the same stream, you know. The Faule Bach. It runs right from the pond over the aqueduct and on to the mill. Then into the moat, on the far side of town. And here we've walked a mile and a half just to catch the same fish we might have caught right at home."

"Ah, but that's no sport—stretching a net across the millrace!"

"That's the spirit! You're right. And the big ones stay in the pond—they're afraid of the wooden aqueduct—except in flood time. If more of them escaped, the townsfolk could catch more."

"You mean anyone can fish in the moat?"

"Not between the Coswigertor and the Elbtor. But in

the other three-fourths, yes. The elector doesn't want too much riffraff milling beneath the palace, even in boats. But that's where the big ones are, or so the fishermen say. The water's nearly seventy feet deep, in spots, and it does harbor some big ones."

"You don't sound much like a proper gamekeeper. Doesn't that go with the fishing rights?"

"It's supposed to, yes. As far as I'm concerned, the duke has more fish and game than he and his court could ever eat. He's generous—I don't mean to belittle him. We who can hunt and fish are expected to share half the bounty, and to police against poachers. Often as not those who can hunt and fish divide their share with the clergy or the poor. But why the poor have to get it like beggars instead of catching it themselves I'll never quite understand. I guess I'm just not a man who believes in the divine right of kings. Without the privileges, my grandfather and I would have been ordinary ditch-diggers. But we were lucky."

Tilman had never thought at length about the laws of feudalism. He realized for the first time that his father, although not wealthy, had been far better off than an ordinary citizen. Tilman did have a few extra gulden in his wallet and a letter of credit on the bank in Torgau.

With the miller at his side he baited a hook, sat cross-legged on the old sluice gate above the weir, and dangled his line into the water. The air overhead was almost still, making just a slight ripple on the water.

"You seen any more of the Tannenlohes, Tilman?"

"No, sir. I should. They probably could use help, after losing all those goods in the millrace. Maybe I can go out some Sunday and help gather hazelnuts or walnuts."

"You sure you don't just want to see Ingi?" The boy blushed to the roots of his tow hair, and the hooknosed fisherman kept on talking. "She's a right smart little filly, to help her mother so much. Almost good enough for a squire's son, I'd say. The villagers might not think so, but I think a village girl is better than a city one."

Tilman yanked as the bobber dove down. With a spray of water a perch skimmed across the surface and arched through the air. Regardless of his spirit the fish was not more than ten inches long, but a good start for the day's sport. Meanwhile Reinhard hooked an eel which was scarcely as thick as his thumb, and threw him back for another day.

The fishermen were both lean and lanky, and although the miller had a ruddier complexion and darker hair the two might have passed for father and son. Tilman felt close enough to his companion to call him Reinhard, dropping the "sir," to the obvious pleasure of the old bachelor.

"Tell me, Reinhard, has the town always felt like this toward Luther?"

"How do you mean, *like this?*"

"Well, as if it's under tension. Waiting for the gun-powder to go off. Not much happening on the surface, but strong undercurrents."

"Hard to say, Tilman. For three years things have been about the same—ever since Luther nailed up the Theses. The students have doubled or tripled. Papal nuncios and chamberlains have been running back and forth. The Saxon Miltitz is worst. He tries to put on pompous airs, but rumor has it he's just an errand boy. Nobody trusts him, neither Luther nor the cardinal."

"The cardinal?"

"Cajetan. He's been commissioned to end Luther's teachings, one way or another. Since Maximilian died, no one knows who holds the cards. The emperor always supported the pope, if there was a question of heresy. But with this new Spanish stripling on the throne, Luther might just get burned at the stake, or poisoned. It's hard to say."

"You think there really is a ban against him? A papal bull, and not just a rumor?"

"I wouldn't be surprised. Cranach says he's heard it from a reliable source—Spalatin, the duke's secretary. But papal politics are hard to figure, and if there's a groschen to be made or lost, I wouldn't try to guess. I do know they've been burning Luther's books all over the map at Meissen, Brandenburg, Leipzig, Merseburg.

Not quite as fast as new ones are printed, but it does show the way the wind's blowing."

"Was it the Theses that started it?"

This time Zillerthal hauled in an eel as thick as his wrist and snuggled it into his pack, almost drooling over the thought of a baked dinner. "Yes and no. The Theses were what flung Luther into the spotlight. He'd been teaching the same thing quietly for years. Then, of course, when he went to Leipzig and debated with Dr. Eck—that really did it. The whole world sat up and took notice."

"When was that?"

"Just last summer. The transcript was shipped off to half a dozen faculties to decide who won. Paris didn't want the honor, saying both men were partially right. Only Louvain and Cologne gave a reply, in favor of Eck, and no one asked those two in the first place."

"That's when the fat hit the fire?"

"Yes. And when the appeal was made to the elector. Mind you, Fredrick didn't say Luther was right, but when the pope ordered him to send the monk straight off to Rome, he refused. Said there'd have to be a hearing first, to determine the issues. Not in Italy, mind you, but in Germany. He said he wouldn't allow any of his professors to leave Saxony unless the emperor—not the pope—guaranteed safe-conduct."

"Sounds like a first-class fight."

"A real difference of opinion, anyway. It's too bad you don't know Luther. He's not a bad sort, certainly not a raging wild boar, a charlatan, an impious heretic, as the Dominicans make him out. The townsfolk adore him, as do the faculty and the councilmen, for the most part. That's why the elector is so loyal, I'm afraid. Not by his own convictions, but because he's influenced by his advisers."

"Is there any danger the elector will weaken?"

"He's a stubborn old soul, and it's hard to say. My guess is no, although Rome can shoot some heavy artillery. Even if he did, Luther probably would be safe if he went north. Both the Duke of Schaumburg and Franz von Sickingen have offered protection, and with a couple of hundred knights against them, Rome would have to shout rather loud."

The creel was growing heavy with fish. Now that the slithering and flapping had lessened, Reinhard Zillerthal spread out the catch on the grassy bank. There were a dozen perch, four good-sized eel, and two carp, one weighing at least five pounds.

"What is it you dislike about our famous monk, Tilman? Sometimes when you talk about Mainz and your love of printing I think you want to leave only because you dislike Luther, and perhaps even Wittenberg."

"It's not the town, so much. Torgau is scarcely better, despite my memories. It's my faith. One doesn't root up everything his parents have planted—a whole way of life. That's what I feel Luther is trying to do, throwing away the good and not replacing it with anything. I'll grant you, there may be good in what he's doing. People get religiously lazy and lose their bearings. But I imagine that in five years Luther will be dead and buried, and the whole church will be better off."

Reinhard shook his head. "I'm not sure. You've met Luther, you've heard him, you've talked with him. You know him, but maybe you don't know the church. Maybe you think it's a place to flip devotional cards or count beads. Maybe you think it's clean and above board, like the protected little priest who says mass in a manor house. It's not like that, Tilman, not when you get out into the great wide world and see what the church really is—immorality, greed, worldliness."

Tilman baited his hook. He was willing to listen to Reinhard, but at the same time he was reserving judgment.

Reinhard poured out the bait, searching for a worm. "I can't *tell* you, but maybe I can *show* you. Ever been to a sodality? A prayer circle, as they're sometimes called? We've had twenty at the Stadtkirche ever since my grandfather's day. They're supposed to be good, pious, God-pleasing societies. The Brotherhood of St. Matthew, the Daughters of the Hearth and Household, the Fraternity of the Precious Blood of the Sacred Heart."

"I know they exist—that's about all."

"Come with me. I haven't gone for years, but I still belong to the Sharpshooters of St. Sebastian and St. Anne. They have a feast tonight at the Bald-faced Stag, on the road to Niemeck. Come along. If you think the church needs no reforming, you're in for quite a shock."

The village of Niemeck was like half a dozen others in the vicinity of Wittenberg. If anything, with scarcely twenty houses and a dozen barns and outbuildings to its credit, it was small. It did have two attractions which sometimes tempted the students and holiday-makers, however: an attractive thirteenth century chapel, beautiful for its simple Norman arches, and the Bald-faced Stag.

The inn was within good walking or posting distance of Wittenberg, just far enough to escape the wary eyes of the town fathers. It dated from the time Niemeck had been a bustling little village, before the growth of Wittenberg and the widening of the road.

The open beams of the roof were blackened with more than a century of smoke, and from one room to the next there was a constant aroma of fine food. For more than an hour Tilman and Reinhard had shared a crowded little table with a retired gunsmith and his wife, pushed so far into the corner they seemed more like on-lookers than participants.

Throughout the inn, on the ground floor and in the balcony, the rafters echoed with boisterous celebrating, and now that the feast of the Sharpshooters was already two hours old, a sodden smell of spilled wine and applewood smoke was replacing the more pleasant odors of roast oxen and lamb.

Tilman, Reinhard, and the old-timers were in a pleasant mood, after such a fine array of food. The oxen had just the right touch of wood smoke, the lamb was delicately flavored with mint. For those who preferred game there was wild duck and creamed eel. The wine had a nutty flavor, and for dessert the banqueters picked at cheese and nuts, in the midst of their merrymaking.

It was the old gunsmith who did most of the talking. Reinhard was happy, because he did not want to influence Tilman needlessly. "I can remember when it was an honor to belong to the Sharpshooters of St. Sebastian and St. Anne." Despite his hoary head his fingers still gave the impression of precision and strength, like the craftsman he was. "I'm not so sure now." He spoke half dreamily, without actually addressing either his wife or the others.

Tilman knew exactly what the gunsmith meant. This wasn't the sporting crowd that liked to go to a goose shoot or a target match. This was an official organization of the church, but to watch them at play did not make one proud, to say the least. Not one in ten was sober

enough to make his way home without falling in a
ditch, and still the leathern tankards flowed with wine.

One cask after another rolled into the rack, where
the serving maids refilled the pitchers and plunked them
on the trestles. Several of the girls had been knocked
coarsely to the floor, either through drunken clumsiness
or the notion that this was what peasant girls were for.

The gunsmith's wife sat shaking her head. She had
enjoyed the meal and the company, to be sure. But now
the banquet was beginning to turn into a riot. The
innkeeper tried to slow the good spirits, but without
success. He finally took things in hand when one of
the revellers called a serving girl bawdy epithets and
tore at her bodice. The innkeeper grasped him by the
shoulders and pushed him toward the door, but not
before a companion had drawn a knife. The blade
flashed through the air, fortunately not with sober aim,
but it caught the host's shirt and a bit of the flesh and
pinned him against a beam. The innkeeper cursed, but
over the noise and roistering no one paid any attention.
He pulled the knife free, hurled it into the blazing fire-
place, and retreated to the kitchen.

"That's enough!" said the gunsmith's wife. "That's
the last straw. And to think this is supposed to be a part
of the church. This is just a ticket for license, not a way
to proclaim the kingdom of God." She was already on

her feet, pulling a shawl about her shoulders. "To-morrow, Martin, you write a letter resigning. I'll no longer be a party to an affair like this."

The elderly couple politely excused themselves and disappeared. Tilman looked sheepishly at his host. "Is it always this bad, Reinhard? Are all the sodalities alike?"

"Pretty nearly, I'm afraid. Not even the priests will come any more. She wasn't far wrong, that woman."

The village clock was striking nine, and Tilman was on his feet. "I've had enough, Reinhard. Let's go."

"I was wondering when you'd get your fill. The real trouble never starts before midnight."

They moved out into the night, with coats and scarves guarding them from the cold. The blanket of clouds had drifted away to reveal a clear and frosty sky.

"Maybe Luther does know what he's doing. Mind you, I'm still far from convinced, but at least I can see his point."

The towers of Wittenberg loomed darkly on the horizon, and the two walked on in silence, lost in their thoughts.

CHAPTER ELEVEN

ULTIMATUM
FROM THE POPE

On the morning of October 10, 1520, except for a ridge of mackerel clouds high off the horizon, the sky was completely clear. For weeks this had been the date Tilman planned to depart for Mainz. He could completely forget the wound in his groin, even when he maneuvered the heavy press. Dr. Pergesius agreed that he was fit enough for a wrestling match.

For two weeks, however, Tilman had not looked forward to the date with so much eagerness as when he lay abed in the dog days of August. By day his mind now was so preoccupied he sometimes lost track of the copy as he sat dreaming over the composing stick. By night he often lay awake thinking of his Torgau days, curious what his mother would say if she were still alive.

He consoled himself that he could postpone the decision for another month and still reach Mainz before the blasts of winter, even if he traveled at leisure and visited all the sights en route. He had consulted nearly all his friends and acquaintances—Cranach, Pergesius, Ingrid, Lotte. Yet he was undecided.

He had already learned so much from Melchior that he began to wonder whether Mainz could really offer more. Cranach bluntly advised him to stay. He could get a job as a journeyman anywhere in Wittenberg.

And although Cranach was not a printer, the many woodcuts he did kept him reasonably up-to-date with the whole trade. In short, Cranach suggested he shouldn't even consider Mainz. Paris maybe, or Venice, but certainly no town in Germany.

In the golden light of dawn Tilman von Rothenau and Eberhard Bostler rounded the corner of the Bürgermeistergasse, half a turning from the little wooden bridge that led across to the Kirchhof and the towers of the Stadtkirche. Though they had known each other less than three weeks, they had become as close as two chestnuts in a single bur.

Eberhard was a year older than his companion. He was a student of law whose father was a well-to-do attorney in Nürnberg. He had dark curly hair, eyes so dark they seemed almost black, a quick tongue, and a mind that demanded respect the minute he opened his mouth. He had happened to come to the Kleins in a way Tilman thought almost providential. With hordes of students flocking from all of Germany to hear the lectures of Luther and Melanchthon, the dormitories soon over-flowed. Even the big bursae of Mercury, Sophia, and the Fountain bulged to the attics, until the townsfolk had begun to take in roomers. Lotte Klein had heard Luther himself make an appeal, after a morning sermon, and gladly volunteered a spare room.

On market days Tilman and Eberhard made it a practice to slip down to the Stadtkirche before they parted for the day, one to the print shop and the other to the classroom. At the request of the elector, Luther had begun to preach not just on festival days but also on market days, when a good many countryfolk congregated in town. Usually the boys also had time to say good morning to Ingrid and to inquire about her family.

The first time the boys had seen Ingrid when they were together, each had been surprised to find that the other knew her, and that the other had once come to her rescue: Eberhard, in lifting her from the Faule Bach, and Tilman in saving her mother from a ducking. Although he was not willing to admit it even to himself, Tilman felt a strange attraction to the girl. The fact that she had made a firm friend in Eberhard meant that he was free to go to Mainz, for now she had a benefactor if her family found itself in more trouble. The danger seemed unlikely, anyway, now that Frater Heidrich had vanished, but Tilman still felt a responsibility.

For more than a week, Tilman had been jealous that there seemed to be a bit more lilt in her voice and a more carefree shrug of her dark locks when she talked with Eberhard than when she talked with him. On market days he made it a point to stop and talk, if there was any excuse to leave the print shop, such as buying ink, collecting a manuscript, paying a bill.

The twin towers of the Stadtkirche loomed impressively even when one stood almost in their shadow. The two spires were joined high overhead by an iron catwalk, so that the watchman and his family could walk from one room to the other. Regularly they tolled the hours of the day, or when someone died, the passing bell. They kept their eyes open for fires, and for bands of robbers, and rang the alarm to warn the townsfolk below.

Unlike the Schlosskirche, which catered to the wealthy, the Stadtkirche was a community church. The shadowy churchyard was pockmarked with hundreds of gravestones, dating to the days when Wittenberg was no more than a trading post for the tribes of the Elbe. Here and there a market girl or a student or a housewife scurried across the Rische Bach and through the limestone portals.

Through the long shadows Tilman watched the sunlight glint off the slate. The church had an odd look of patchwork. The old chancel at one time had been a tiny chapel, and the stones of the nave were enough different in color from those of the towers to indicate several different centuries of construction. Over the chancel an airy gothic plume pointed toward the heavens, as if to show the priest the direction of his prayers.

As usual there was a good-sized crowd inside, despite the early hour. Two years earlier Luther had added the preaching duties at the Stadtkirche to his schedule, ever since the old priest became ill. Gradually those who came to worship had increased from a tiny handful to nearly a churchful.

Though the Stadtkirche was not nearly so impressive as the Schlosskirche, it did have a solemn atmosphere and considerable artistry. The bronze font, weighing more than eight men could lift, was an outstanding work of art, with statues of the apostles cleverly cast beside those of griffons and dragons and birds of prey.

Usually Luther preached from the tiny little pulpit off the transept, which his broad shoulders made seem even smaller, but occasionally he appeared at the *Flügelaltar.* Here he was overshadowed by a vast portrait of the Virgin Mary, the church's guardian and namesake.

The few pews near the front and along the sides had long ago been claimed by infirm old women and mothers with infants. Tilman and Eberhard stood beside the pillars of the portico.

Despite Luther's new kind of preaching, there was a strong feeling of antiquity about St. Mary's, as if the walls had once sheltered St. Peter or St. Paul. A few townsfolk superstitiously contended the pigeons fluttering about the towers were actually the souls of the dead.

Funeral brasses set into the floor showed where previous priests and dukes lay buried, waiting the last trumpet in God's own house. Thousands of feet had worn the brasses smooth, and but for the church register no one would have known who was buried there.

As usual Luther read a long portion from the Scriptures and then set about his exposition. Unlike many preachers, he considered the sermon important and did not give just a pious retelling of the life of St. Sebastian or an allegory about a fox with a religious application. He stood there in the plain black habit of a friar, his face earnest, although his voice showed he was not really so grave. Oddly enough, he was preaching on the parable of the Pharisee and the Publican.

He talked chiefly of the kind of Pharisees one might find in any German city. He was careful not to mention Wittenberg, lest he hurt anyone, but he did paint a true-to-life picture of those who might be considered Pharisaic: the cloth merchant who wanted to be highly thought of but never bothered to share a pfennig with

the poor; the greedy friar more interested in the price
of a mass than in the care of a soul; the money-lender
who would rather see a poor widow rot in jail than
give her an extra week to repay a loan.

The faces of those who had gathered to worship
showed rapt attention. It was as if Luther were pointing
the finger directly at people they knew and, although
they might not confess it publicly, directly at them. But
he did not simply scourge them, like a stern judge. He
also pictured God's plan of salvation. No matter how
black they saw themselves, even as the worst of Pharisees, God could forgive them still, through the cross.

For Tilman the living voice of Luther was spellbind-
ing, even though he had set sermon after sermon in
type, proofed it, seen it through the press and sewn
the pages. To hear Luther in person was far more stirring
than simply to read him. Somehow, in the presence of
the crippled grandmothers and the legless veterans, the
Gospel came alive, and the tears on the faces of the
elderly sometimes stirred the consciences of the young
who prided themselves on their intellectualism.

The monk spoke briefly, as he almost always did on
market days when a class of students awaited him at the
Augustinerkloster. The worshipers filed out into the
little square between the Stadtkirche and the City Hall.
What the preacher had said struck home, and most of

them moved quietly and thoughtfully. There was no buzz of conversation about how fine the sermon had been; the hearers thought about it rather than talked about it.

A look at the clock showed Tilman and Eberhard they had time to linger. Ingi's stall was scarcely out of the way for either of them, and even if it had been, they would nevertheless have found an excuse to stop. They swung quickly across the cobblestones of the square.

"Good morning, little nightingale," trilled Eberhard. Tilman envied him, always so aggressive in his courtesies.

Ingi was scarcely taken aback. "Am I as black-feathered as that?" Her laugh showed it was all in jest. "Or do I lay my eggs in a strange nest and then fly away— no, that's the cuckoo, isn't it?"

In the lightning exchanges between Bostler and Ingrid, Tilman always felt at a loss. He never had considered himself worldly-wise, and although he could talk to the girl sensibly enough when they were alone, it was not easy in the presence of others. For Eberhard it seemed simple, as if he had done it all his life, and he never needed to stop to think of a reply.

"How was the sermon this morning, Tilman?"

"Prima. I've never heard Dr. Luther in better form. I think I could recite it almost by heart."

"I wish you would. If it weren't for the cart, I could hear him myself. But I'd better stay with it, after all we lost last month."

Tilman glanced at the clock on the town hall. "Maybe I can tell you at noon what he said, if I have to pick up the vellum. Mind, I may not remember everything." He was so serious and so bashful that the girl smiled.

Her stall was nearly empty, compared with the bounty displayed in the summer. There were turnips, apples, beets, cabbages, carrots, a few eggs, cheeses, and nuts—whatever could be sheltered from the frost or buried for a month beneath straw and sand. The market slowed noticeably in the autumn and winter, although, of course, it was an excellent time for butchering. Of mutton and pork, of sausage and ham, there was considerably more than in the heat of July.

Because of the cold the shopping moved at a quicker pace. Housewives no longer stood and haggled. If the price seemed fair, they bought. Making a full round to compare prices and then returning to the cheapest was not nearly so popular now that there was a touch of frost in the air.

With the university in session the students en route to classes far outnumbered the early shoppers. Some headed eastward up the Collegiengasse to the cloister; others trod westward to the school of law and the library.

Tilman cast a wary eye at the Rathaus clock. In ten minutes he would have to be at the print shop, and he debated inwardly whether he could afford to stay longer than Eberhard. Normally it was touch and go. It was almost as if Ingrid would think best of the one who left last.

"How long do you think they'll let Luther go on preaching, Eberhard?" The girl twisted packs of roasted chestnuts, a favorite food for youngsters when their mothers brought them to market. "What do the professors say?"

"Nothing specific, Ingi. The whole town's afire with rumors. Spalatin says the bull's already signed, and once it arrives, Luther's days are numbered. The vicar-general will certainly have to silence his public preaching, at least until there's been a hearing. Then, if he's lucky, he may go right on. The hearing will not be for a year or two, of course."

High up on the Marienkirche a bell began to toll. Its tempo was quick, like an alarm, but it spoke softly, not like Old Nick and the ham-size clappers. The doves from the tower flapped excitedly, swirling away from the din of the bell.

On the Coswigertor a watchman hallooed down to the drawbridge. A rumble of horse's hooves echoed sharply over the timbers. Schoolboys scooted out of the way as a courier's mount trotted briskly through the Coswigergasse. The man rode erect on his black gelding, like the emissary of a king, but the silver and black trappings, together with his livery and pennon, proclaimed him nuncio of the archbishop of Trier. The bridle was bright with the sparkle of silver, and a scarlet saddle blanket peeked out from under the leather. His horse had the look of frequent currying, with a glossy coat and mane clipped and curled. He bore himself so disdainfully and with so little concern for the onlookers that he might have stepped from another world.

Without passing directly through the market he reined his mount sharply across the far side of the square, worked his way over the stone bridge to the Collegiengasse, and turned toward the Black Cloister. With curious eyes the people in the square stared after him, and schoolboys actually took up the chase at a safe and respectful distance.

A whirlpool of leaves and dust spun behind the courier. Scarcely was he out of sight when the sound of running feet broke the silence. It was Old Jack, the town crier, shaking his little handbell as if to announce Judgment Day, and trying to clutch in his free hand a scroll of paper and his three-cornered hat.

His leather jacket showed the strains of many a rain and snow, but today the town fathers were more interested in his news than in how he looked. For once they cared little whether Wittenberg's crier made a fine impression on travelers and merchants.

"Hear ye, hear ye," cried Old Jack over the fierce tinkling of his bell, "hear ye, hear ye." He mounted the steps of the gallows two risers at a time and stood quivering at the brink of the platform.

Ingi, Tilman, and Eberhard approached the platform, within easy hearing but still where they could keep a sharp watch on the stall. "The nuncio of the archbishop!" the crier kept shouting, with a finger stretched toward the direction in which the courier had disappeared into the court of the Augustinian monastery.

"He's probably summoning Luther," said Eberhard, without raising his voice. "Just as they did John Hus." Ingi looked at her companions. A shadow of concern played over her face.

"You don't think the emperor has died, do you?"

Tilman answered in a whisper. "There's no passing bell. Remember how it was when Maximilian died?"

The girl nodded. "That's so, Tilman. Even in the villages we got word at once."

The crier strained until his voice rasped. Shopkeepers came running from doors on all sides of the square. "A bull from His Highness Leo, through his servant the archbishop of Trier. Martin Luther, the Augustinian monk, is placed under the ban. He is to appear in Rome in sixty days, or he forfeits all rights. Already his books have been burned and unless he recants he may be too. Hear ye, hear ye."

Old Jack lumbered down from the gallows, unrolled a copy of the scroll against the brass-studded door of the town hall, and hammered the tacks home. Once his job was done, he proceeded to the far corner of the square, his bell tolling for silence, and began his spiel anew.

As soon as the crowd saw that the scroll was in Latin, they crowded after the crier. Leaving the girl behind, Tilman worked his way to the door. "Exsurge, Domine," the announcement began, in a florid chancery hand. "Arise, O Lord, and judge Thine own cause."

Tilman skimmed the notice quickly, with Eberhard reading over his shoulder. The document pinpointed Luther's heresies and ordered him to cease writing and teaching. If he did not wish to travel to Rome personally, he could send a sealed confession by the hand of fellow monks.

In the most formal tone, as one king would write to another, the bull summed up Luther's failings and compared him with heretics of the past. Though the copy there on the oaken door bore no seal or ribbons, it did bear a legal signature—Leo, bishop of Rome, servant of the servants of God.

CHAPTER TWELVE

AFTERNOON AMBUSH

Ingrid Tannenlohe dropped a handful of hazelnuts into the leather pouch and warmed her fingers against the soft goat hair of her scarf. On such an icy day, Tilman examined the scarf with care because it represented the homey virtues he admired in Ingrid. With her own hand, according to her mother, Ingi had sheared the goats and carded the wool, spun the yarn and knitted the cloth. Although every country girl was reasonably skilled at cooking and sewing, at fifteen Ingrid already seemed a past master of the arts of homemaking. The scarf was an ell square. After folding it into a triangle, she crossed the doubled ends beneath her chin and still had enough fringe to warm the hands. Tilman

157

hoped the girl was not so frozen as he was, picking hazelnuts when two inches of snow blanketed the ground and a cold gale blew off the Baltic.

The kernels nudged tightly against the hulls, and with gloves it was almost impossible to do a proper job of shelling them. Either hull and all went into the bag, which of course filled it far too quickly and caused weight and waste, or else the gloved fingers let the nuts slip away into the snow.

They joked about hazelnuts, and despite the cold it was fun. For one thing, it made a good excuse to slip away to the river and talk. The cottage was pleasant enough, but in two tiny rooms, with many brothers and sisters they could never feel alone. Neither had connived to escape from the house; Ingi's mother had suggested it. A little brother, Peterli, and his collie Ruffles came along too.

The swamplands grew dense with willows and hazel. The air had been frigid for a week, and although there was an inch of ice on the potholes, the level of the river had dropped, leaving air pockets and thin ice. The rule, Tilman kept telling the boy, was to skip the trees near the river. Even if the wind had already knocked off the nuts, they would just have to rot in the snow. Not even a basketful was worth the risk of a ducking in this temperature.

The three of them were down on a gentle slope,

scarcely a hundred yards from the cottage. Without foliage, Kronberg seemed smaller than ever. The houses were scattered piecemeal along the Torgau road, with three or four down toward the Elbe. A trickle of smoke wafted from the Tannenlohe cottage, and Tilman anticipated the hot drink the widow Tannenlohe would have waiting when they came shivering through the wattle door.

In the churchyard nearby the snow on the yews and the graves looked like a Christmas scene or a black and white landscape from the pen of Albrecht Dürer. It was mid-afternoon on a Sunday, St. Martin's Day. The cold was really quite appropriate, Ingrid had suggested jokingly when Tilman arrived. After all, wasn't it on a day like this that Martin of Tours gave a shivering beggar half his cloak and earned a niche among the saints?

The ice on the millpond was quite safe, and four or five youngsters slid about on their wooden skates. Tilman rubbed his hands inside his jacket, in the hope of restoring the circulation.

"Tell me, Ingi, where did you get the dye for your shawl? Henna from the apothecary's?"

"No, silly!" She laughed. "Countryfolk can't afford henna. Besides, it's too orange. This is from the roots of cedar and hemlock, boiled up. That's what makes the streams red, the charcoal burners say—all those roots dangling in the water."

Peterli and Ruffles had drifted over toward the pond to romp with the skaters. Tilman found it pleasant to have the girl nearby, even when she said nothing. He had never thought he, the son of a squire, would have anything in common with an ordinary village girl. But he did enjoy her company, and when he had not seen her for a week he missed her.

Tilman did not delve too deeply into his affection for Ingi. Ever since they had stood in the market and watched the arrival of the bull he knew he would have to reach a decision concerning both Wittenberg and Ingi. He had dallied for a month already. If he did not make up his mind soon, the full blast of winter would cover the land.

Another big problem was the print shop. Melchior had far more copy than he could ever set in type, more than the other printers. Although Melchior would be sorry to lose a worker as good as Tilman, he realized he had no hold on the lad. As his brother-in-law Lucas kept telling him, he should be thankful for small blessings, and rejoice that the apprentice had already done so much.

As for Ingrid, Tilman's quandary was equally difficult. He did like the girl's spunk, her smiling face, her courage, her faith, her devotion to her family, her concern for the smaller ones. A country girl, she had nearly reached the age for marrying, but Tilman was neither of a mind nor an age to think of wedlock. It was true he still had his letter of credit for forty gulden, but this he considered a nest egg for a print shop, not for buying a house or taking a wife. Until he had a job and a regular income, and knew what he wanted to do and where he wanted to do it, marriage was out of the question.

His religious problem also bothered him. He was strangely troubled by the teachings of Luther. The evening he had spent in the monk's study and the many mornings in the Stadtkirche had warmed his heart more than he liked to admit. On the other hand, if the Holy Father really considered Luther a heretic, and if the bishops and cardinals all agreed, then Luther must be in the wrong. He had thought long and hard while walking to Kronberg. There were few travelers on the road and it had been a good afternoon for thinking. What troubled him, although he could not really lay his finger on it, was his faith.

Somehow he loved more than he could express the old ways he had learned as a boy from his mother and from the Brothers of the Common Life. He was awed by the incense, the candles, the statues, the confessional, the processions, the elaborate garb, the plainsong, the polished mitre, the glitter of a reliquary, the monstrance.

His indecision was not merely between the old and the new. Why couldn't he have both? Why couldn't

the church worship in more ways than one? Why did
the path of faith have to be so narrow, so exclusive?

Most of what Luther said, Tilman found to be true,
otherwise his decision would have been easy. There
were faults in the church. The simple folks *did* tend to
worship relics or statues even though the priests (most of
them) truly worshiped God. A woodcutter sometimes
did buy an indulgence as a license to get drunk. The
bishops *did* barter their palliums. A pope or two *had*
won positions through politics. Many a cardinal *was* lax
in his morals. A country shepherd often *did* know as
much about his Savior as did a priest. Church and people
were woefully ignorant and poor and oppressed.

But was this really the fault of the church, as Luther
argued? Could it not have been the fault of the times:
illiteracy, taxes, lack of roads, poor education, disease?
The whole empire seemed to be falling apart now that
the Turks were invading the Balkans. And in the midst
of all this, Martin Luther gave the impression not of
building up the church but of tearing it down.

When he was a youngster Tilman's mother had always talked of the devil as something real and fearful.
Sometimes, she had said, Lucifer appeared in the most
mild and pleasant disguise, as an emperor, a priest, a
virgin, an infant. No matter how good something appeared, it could be rotten within. This was somewhat the
way Tilman viewed Luther. Even if the poor and un-

learned were hesitant and confused, a squire ought to have the good sense to discern the truth. He had an obligation.

Was Luther really just a simple Bible scholar? Was he just another prior who ran a monastery? Was he just a professor? Or was there something of the devil in him? Was he really scheming to overthrow the kingdom of God? Did he really alienate the hearts of the faithful, like Absalom who stood at the gate and deceitfully won over the followers of his father David?

High overhead the crows were holding a raucous conference, but Tilman was so lost in his thoughts that he paid no attention either to the crows or to the hazelnuts. Inside his jacket he pounded his fingers until they felt warm. Ingi, who had moved thirty or forty steps nearer the river, noticed his frown.

"Cold, Tilman? Mother'll soon have the cakes done, so we'd better call Peterli and head for the house."

"Sorry. Just thinking." The bag over his shoulder hung heavy with nuts, and the weight called him back to reality.

"With Peterli's, even if he has only a handful, we have twenty or thirty pounds. That's a full day's work, even when the sun is bright. That'll buy enough cloth for three or four shirts, and a skirt for mother to boot."

They cut diagonally across the churchyard toward the pond. Peterli stood warming his hands by an open fire, not far from the shore, with two or three of the skaters. Ruffles bounded after a hare up the millrace, but lost it in the maze of stones in the churchyard.

They had scarcely reached the road when a figure raced up from the distance, followed by a second. The man in the lead was so out of breath he could say nothing at first. He slowed to a walk. "Help, help! The guards! Call the guards!" With that he raced on, veering toward the footbridge across the Elbe.

Beyond the ragged line of firs, where the dark trace of the road bent to the east along the river, the light of a fire glowed in the somber sky. Pillars of smoke eddied in the wind, and the glare of flames burst up through the gathering dusk. The fire was at least a quarter of a mile away, and just beginning to break out into billowing flames. It seemed to rise from the road itself or at least close by. The smoldering smoke indicated that a barn full of hay was on fire.

The little huddle of youngsters on the pond did not know what to make of the stranger's message. Only Tilman and Ingrid were old enough to be responsible. Tilman barked out orders almost as soon as the situation made sense. "Peterli, you and the rest stay in Kronberg. We cannot risk having you burned. Ingrid, you make sure they stay here. Get them to go from door to door. Maybe we can round up enough manpower to save the barn, or at least the other buildings. Get as many men as you can, as quickly as you can. I'll run ahead."

With that, Tilman bounded into action. His lithe limbs took him past the churchyard almost as if he were flying. There was enough gravel poking up through the snow to give him fair footing. The padding of snow dulled the sound of his boots, and as he raced through the gathering dusk toward the patch of flame, he thought he was floating through a dream. Only the chill air and the blood coursing through his cold cheeks reminded him he was conscious.

In the half-light he could see four or five figures racing out across the countryside. A moment later a band of horsemen galloped off to the east along the Torgau road, a quarter of a mile away. He tried to figure out what was happening. A youth ran directly toward him, shouting. "Run, run, run for your life! It's highwaymen!"

Tilman caught the young fellow by the shoulders and stopped him. "What's happened? Take your time. No one's chasing you. What's happened? You're quite safe. There's no reason to act like a frightened rabbit."

The youth tried to shake free. Tilman's fingers clung tight. The boy resigned himself to his fate. "I was with the train, twelve wagons of furs and linen bound from Warsaw to Frankfurt. Then highwaymen attacked us— twenty or thirty, at least, and armed to the teeth with halberds, swords, crossbows. They dragged a log across the road, and once we stopped they galloped out from the trees."

"Did they hurt you?"

"Me, no. But they killed Herr Kimpel. He tried to hide his purse. And Dominick got a bad cut. He was hiding in a wagon and hoped they wouldn't spot him. The rest of us escaped, far as I know."

"What happened to the train? Did they take everything?"

"Mostly just the money. And the load of ermine. The linens and woolens they spat on. There were only ten or twelve haulers, not counting the merchants. We never had a chance."

"To look at you run you didn't put up much of a fight."

"You wouldn't either, against crossbows and swords. Not when they struck down the master right before your eyes, and his blood ran red in the snow."

Tilman shook the lad, who was still shivering with fright. The wagons were only two or three hundred yards away, burning fiercely. Two or three at the far end loomed up dark and gaunt against the horizon. "Come on. Not along the road, though." He scooted behind a hedgerow. "Quiet. I saw at least a score take off in the opposite direction, riding as if the devil were on their heels."

They skirted a row of apple trees along a small rill. They were close enough to see the spouts of flame shoot into the sky, to smell the acrid smoke of burning fur, and to hear the wild neighing of the horses, many still shackled to the overturned wagons. A mare, her mane outlined in flame, broke free, crashed through the hedgerow, and dashed madly across the meadow. Two or three men lay groaning in the road. One crawled weakly in the circle of firelight.

Tilman pushed his way through the thorns. He peered the length of the train. Five or six wagons had been driven together, overturned, and set afire. "Come on!" His voice was quiet but demanding. The boy was reluctant. "Come on, stupid. Let's save what we can." Tilman dragged his companion through the ditch.

The heat of the flames warmed his cheeks and put a sparkle in his eye. There was no time for pausing. He pulled a knife from his belt and went into action. One cart, just beginning to smolder, lay near the flaming holocaust. He cut the horse's traces as it whinnied in pain. A red slash showed where the sword had struck through the hamstrings.

"Now! The cart is free and the horse is beyond help. Grab the singletree. Twist. Now the wagon bed. That's right. Rock it. B-a-c-k-a-n-d-f-o-r-t-h. That's right. Now hard!" The cart righted itself and rocked to its wheels. "Harder!" They grunted as the cart rolled backward.

With his muscles straining, the frightened boy calmed. "There's nothing more we can save," Tilman told him. "The fire's too hot." One or two of the haulers were drifting back to the wagons. Their eyes glowed like those of wild beasts in the circle of firelight.

"Listen, boy!" Tilman spoke quickly and sharply. "Someone has to notify the authorities. Maybe they can call out the guard before the highwaymen escape. That's my job—I know the shortcut to the Elstertor. You stay here and care for the injured. Keep them warm, try to stanch the bleeding. See, there's help coming already. From Kronberg." He pointed to half-a-dozen figures silhouetted against the snow. "You can take the injured to the farmhouse there. Mind you, don't run off again. The highwaymen are gone and somebody has to stay. That's your job, what your master pays you for. When I get back, I want everyone to speak well of what you've done—understand?"

Without waiting for an answer Tilman crashed through the hedgerow and set out for Wittenberg. He loped along at a steady trot, knowing just where the creeks and low places made the footing treacherous. The cloud cover had scudded away, and in the light of the stars he made quick time. In ten minutes he was abreast of the duke's fishpond, and in another two or three his boots clattered on the planks of the drawbridge. "Halloo," he shrieked at the guard on the turret, "open the gate." The iron portcullis had been swung into place, blocking the path. "Let me in! Call out the guard. There's been an attack on a merchant train."

The watchman peered curiously at the winded boy. Against the snow Tilman appeared as a black silhouette. The guard said not a word. In the dark shadows behind the grating he talked anxiously. A panel of grillwork clicked from a heavy key, and then slid open. Three guards stepped through. With them was the man Tilman had first seen on the Kronberg common, sounding a warning. They stared at the youth suspiciously. Two guards grabbed him by the shoulders, and another lifted a lantern high, shedding its rays over his face. "That's one of them!" shouted the merchant. "I swear it!" He pulled off Tilman's cap and spread open his collar. "I'd recognize that tow hair and the long thin nose anywhere. Even the cleft in the chin. He's the one! He's the one who killed Kimpel."

Before he could grasp what was happening Tilman felt his arms pinioned and the rough fibers of a rope cutting fiercely into his wrists. They jerked both hands behind his back and tied them tightly.

"We ought to throw him right into the moat," said one of the guards. "Serve him right." He slugged him hard on the shoulder, and the boy went skidding over the icy boards. The black water stared him in the face and he felt himself falling. He felt a sharp pain in his wrist. He had one leg over the edge of the moat when they yanked him back. "It would save the taxpayers a couple loaves of bread if we didn't have to feed him before the hanging."

The rope stung and burned. Tilman stumbled against the portcullis. "Climb through, highwayman. See if you like a taste of cold iron." He swatted him with the flat of a sword. Tilman winced. His shoulder ached as if it had cracked.

"Let me talk, let me talk. I'm no highwayman. I'm Tilman von Rothenau. I work in Master Melchior's print shop. I just ran back to call the guards. I was in Kronberg all the time—the Tannenlohes can tell you."

"Save your breath, son," said the guard. "You'll have your chance in court. This man says you're a highwayman. He was there. It was his brother you killed. The guard is already on the road. Why didn't you meet them?"

"I took the hunter's trail through Wildrosen."

"A likely story. Probably just got separated from the brigands and didn't know where else to flee, in all the excitement. Thought you could slip back to the print shop."

The merchant spoke again. "I couldn't possibly be mistaken. It was still a bit light. I got a good look. Same kind of coat, hair, eyes, chin. Everything."

The guard nodded. On either side, they dragged their

prisoner up the stone steps to the guardhouse. The limestone was slippery, and more than once he barked his shins against the masonry. A heavy iron door clanged open. The top was of grillwork, and the bottom of solid metal.

He felt himself hurled against the wall, four or five feet inside the door, and fell hard on the cold rock. A pile of snow had sifted into the corner, spotlighted by a stray beam of light from a flare outside. The door clanged shut and clicked. His wrists ached from the bite of the rope, his shoulder stung from the blow of the sword, his head reeled from the crash against the wall.

Half stunned, he wondered how soon he would freeze to death. That, at least, would be a slight improvement over a watery grave in the moat, or death by hanging on the town gibbet.

CHAPTER THIRTEEN

ERROR AND REWARD

Tilman von Rothenau rolled over on the icy bricks and groaned. A firm hand grasped his shoulder. He tried to shake free. His head whirled. Was he in the depths of Hades, being pounded to death by the sledge-hammers of impish blacksmiths? But in the forge of hell one would at least be warm, and here he was cold, deadly cold, stiff with cold.

After considerable effort he managed to shake his head and focus his eyes. Every muscle ached. He looked again. He saw no jailkeeper. What surprised him even more, he did not even see the Prince of Devils. Instead, buried beneath a heavy cowl, was the nondescript face of a monk. He looked once more, this time almost in de-

172

spair. Then he relaxed. Framed in the cowl was the face of Martin Luther.

The friar was almost as astonished as Tilman. "Tilman! What are *you* doing here?"

It was some time before the apprentice was able to prop himself on his elbows and gather his wits. Had he been a common drunk or petty thief, he would have expected the monk's visit, for Luther made it his duty at least once a week to shrive the prisoners. Occasionally, while the public hangman waited, Luther offered the last rites.

Tilman's feelings as he gradually roused from his frozen stupor were not far from those of a man who has risen from the grave. The walls of the city jail were scarcely more hospitable than those of the guardhouse, but at least they kept off the snow.

"Herr Doktor!" They were the first words Tilman was able to speak. "Where am I?" The sound was so weak and so quavering Luther showed a sign of concern.

"In the city jail, Tilman. They brought in four or five of the highwaymen last night . . . . But surely you're not one of . . . "

Gradually Tilman began to remember the events of the night, though he was still not steady enough to sit up. "No, Herr Pfarrer. They think I am, but I'm not. I spent the whole afternoon with Ingrid Tannenlohe. Once they question Ingrid, I'll be in the clear. Last night, though, I thought I was a goner. They dangled me half-way off the drawbridge, and I could nearly touch the icy moat."

Luther took the boy's face between his hands. One eye was badly swollen, and there were bruises and scratches everywhere. With the sleeve of his habit he daubed at a smear of dirt and blood. "Turnkey, trunkey!" A guard came running so quickly he might have feared the monk was being throttled. "Take us to the captain of the guard. This lad is no highwayman."

The grillwork swung open to the click of a key and the guard led the way up a flight of stairs. Luther helped Tilman lower himself to the bench before a roaring fire. The guard excused himself. "Call if you need me, Lord Abbot. I'll be in the hallway. The captain is questioning a prisoner. I'll tell him you want to see him."

"I do indeed." Tilman fumbled with the buttons of his jacket, but his numbed fingers could not undo them. The monk solicitously loosened the bindings and smoothed his shirt. A bit of color came back to the boy's cheeks. "How'd they ever catch you, anyway? At Kronberg? Can anyone else testify where you were?"

"Just Ingi and Peterli. Oh, and there was a youth. An apprentice, I imagine. I met him running away, and ordered him back. He'd surely remember me."

"Where was it they laid hands on you?"

"At the Coswigertor. Sorry. The Elstertor. I'm not

thinking straight. There was a merchant who'd escaped. He took one look and said I was one of them. The guards beat me half senseless."

"Didn't you protest?"

"I told them who I was, but they didn't believe me. He claimed he couldn't be mistaken. The color of my hair. The cleft in my chin. The jacket. The long lean nose. I'm supposed to be the leader, the one who did the killing."

"No wonder they were rough. Ah, but I hear footsteps. We'll soon get to the bottom of this and have you released."

The captain strode through the doorway, a short, square-shouldered man with the rigid backbone of a soldier. "Dr. Luther, a pleasure. But why do you waste your time with scoundrels like this?" He looked at Tilman scornfully.

"But Captain Jörg, there's been a mistake. This lad's no murderer. I know him. He's an apprentice in the Klein print shop. I've often had dealings with him."

The captain squinted sourly. "That's not what the merchant said, Herr Doktor. Described him right to his cap." Despite the scorn, he examined the prisoner. Tilman's face was a mass of dirt and bruises. The captain's eyes took on a puzzled look, then a grin, and finally an outright burst of laughter. He reached for the tiny bell on his desk and rang it fiercely. Within twenty seconds

"You picked the wrong day to go courting."

three guards came running. He whispered, and they disappeared. "Odd," said the captain. "Good thing they didn't feed him to the carp."

A shuffle of footfalls sounded in the hall, and a lanky figure strutted in, with a guard on either side. Luther and Tilman reacted almost together. "Turk Stutzer!" The prisoner's face was downcast and his eyes bloodshot, but there was no doubt that it was the medical student from Frankfurt, long sought by the town fathers for inciting to riot.

The captain stood him beside Tilman. The two boys resembled each other. Turk was at least two inches taller, and his body not so agile and athletic, but in facial features alone they might have passed for brothers, or at least cousins, with their long, thin noses, cleft chins, and mops of linen hair over their foreheads. The saber scar on Turk's cheek made him look older and fiercer, but the overall resemblance was undeniable.

Luther smiled. "You picked the wrong day to go courting, Tilman."

The captain turned to the guard. "Bring in Kimpel, from the Golden Cockerel. At once, even if you have to drag him out of bed. Understand?"

"Yes, sir!" The guard took a cape from the rack and without slowing trotted down the hall.

The captain took off Tilman's jacket and examined his head and shoulders. "Do you want a doctor, boy?"

"I don't think so, sir. They can't cure stiffness, can they?"

"You're lucky you're young. In two days the aches will be gone. And we're lucky you're alive, or there'd be the devil to pay from the elector."

"And from me," Luther added.

"The whole town, I fear. Herr Kimpel must be more careful where he points an accusing finger."

The clock in the town hall was striking eight when the guard dragged a sleepy merchant up the stairway.

The captain herded him near the settle and lined up Turk and Tilman in the sunlight. A look of bewilderment crossed the merchant's face.

"It's the one on the left, captain. I couldn't be mistaken." Tilman winced. "But no! I *am* mistaken. The murderer had a scar. I remember seeing it when he struck down my brother. He really knew how to swing a saber—like a dragoon." A deep blush crossed the merchant's face. "Then this other lad—he really was telling the truth?"

"He really was telling the truth. It was *you* who got him thrown into jail and nearly got him killed."

The merchant rubbed his hands sheepishly. "Then you *did* want to warn the guard?"

"Yes, sir. You raced through the village of Kronberg, sir. Remember the boy and girl by the pond, where you slowed to yell for help? That was me."

The flustered merchant had lost all his defiance. "But you're not the young man that caught my son and raced back to the wagon train, are you?"

"Yes, sir."

"May the good Lord have mercy."

"On us all," said Luther.

"My son—in all the confusion I'd lost him. But you looked after him. Saved a whole wagon of fur, too, worth two hundred gulden. Though it doesn't make up for your suffering, you'll be pleased to know I'd offered a reward of two gulden for anyone who could find you —the boy who helped my boy."

The words of the merchant flowed out so spontaneously and penitently the captain hesitated to scold him. "Let's just be thankful he's still alive. You'll have to be more careful, Herr Kimpel."

"I'm indeed sorry. Let me do what I can for the boy. It could have been worse. I'll see to it that he gets the best medical care in Wittenberg, and a new suit of clothing. After a night in jail, his is a little the worse for wear. It doesn't look warm enough, anyway. You said you were a printer's apprentice?"

"Yes, sir. A helper, at any rate, though I'm not formally apprenticed." Tilman looked tired and exhausted, though a flicker of life was returning to his eyes. His fingers were warming now, which made them ache more.

"Don't think I'm not grateful, lad. What's left of the caravan will still bring me a profit." The merchant was coming fully awake. "Tell you what I'll do. I offered two gulden for anyone who could find you. I'll add that to what I should give *you*. Twelve instead of ten. Is that satisfactory, seeing I had to discover you the hard way?"

"It appears to me," said the captain, "Tilman had the hard way. But at least he hasn't been forgotten."

This time Tilman answered. "Thank you, Herr Kimpel. But I can't take a reward. I only did my duty."

"Mind you, Tilman, this has nothing to do with the mistaken identity. This is something I would have done anyway. I'm not trying to cover up what I did. I'm sorry. I just want to reward you for saving the furs. There's enough ermine to keep my shops in business for a year, and I have you to thank for saving it." The merchant paused, casting an anxious look toward the monk. "If you think twelve gulden too much for a boy, Lord Abbot, perhaps we can set up a trust until he is of age, with you as guardian, or perhaps his master, if you prefer."

Tilman protested a reward in any form, but Luther caught his eye and quieted his complaints. Tilman yielded, thinking of Ingi and the printing shop. "Thank you, sir. I'll try to spend it wisely, so you won't regret it. Thank you."

CHAPTER FOURTEEN

THE BURNING
OF THE BULL

The fire in the grate cast a red glow over the whole
print shop, and to a stranger, Master Melchior's estab-
lishment might have looked like a furnace in hell, with
apprentice devils, journeymen devils, and master devils
all turning out the worst kind of printed devilry for His
Satanic Majesty.

In the strange glow, Printer's Devil Tilman von Rothenau displayed a black smear across the cheek. A new
apprentice had made the mistake of using water instead
of oil on a woodcut. Not more than a dozen sheets
were lost, fortunately, but someone did have to clean the
press and give the water a chance to dry, lest it smudge
the whole day's run.

With copy heaped head high on the compositor's desk, Tilman doubted if there would be any let-up before Christmas. The journeymen who lived nearby wanted at least a short break for the holidays, now that the Feast of St. Nicholas was past, but Melchior did not see how he could possibly give them more than four or five days. Here it was December 10 and already three or four weeks of printing had been set in type and was waiting to be run.

Like every other printer in Wittenberg Melchior needed more space, more help, and more machines. The university and the court kept pouring manuscripts onto his desk. He could have used a second press and six more journeymen, if the money and the room were available. His tiny storehouse already bulged to the walls with men and paper.

He especially wanted a font of roman type. His gothic type, even though it was beginning to show wear from six months of use, was still the finest in Wittenberg. But if he could buy roman matrices and have them cast by a skilled goldsmith, he would be twice as well equipped as any printer in town.

Deep in his heart, which was not very far from his pocketbook, he realized there was more money in turning out a quality book with quality type and quality paper than in being a mere duplicator, producing nothing but cheap pamphlets and placards.

In the rush Tilman had been too busy to think of leaving for Mainz. If he could have made up his mind definitely, the step would have been easier. However, he did not want to desert his master in the busiest time of the year, and to some degree he hesitated leaving at all. In fact, he would have welcomed a heavy snowfall, for that would surely have cut off all chance of travel and forced him to spend the winter in Wittenberg.

Ever since the robbery he had been a local hero. Ingi's brothers, although they had not been directly involved, eyed him as if he were Samson or Hercules. The town council struck a silver medallion and presented it formally in the presence of the company of printers. Sybil, the elector's wife, wrote in her own hand an elaborate note of praise for clearing the city of ruffians and making it safe for women and children, for defending a market girl, and for aiding in the brigands' capture.

The finest tribute was a purse of five golden gulden sealed to a note from the elector. That was a tribute he could use if he ever had a chance to start a print shop. He deposited it and the reward from Herr Kimpel with the comptroller, for fear it might be stolen.

The robbery had not had purely evil results. The guards had captured all the highwaymen. The last to fall to their custody were two peasants, already in difficulty with their landlords, and Frater Heidrich. The

Dominican had been caught hiding in a haymow. As he drew his sword the guards shot him dead with a bolt from a crossbow. As one of the ringleaders, along with Turk Stutzer, Frater Heidrich probably would have been hanged if he had been caught alive. As it was, his order defrocked him, even after his death.

At least his clerical garb did save him one ignominy. His beheaded body did not hang, like Turk Stutzer's, from a leafless ash tree outside the city gate, nor his unseeing eyes stare from a pike atop the watchtower as a warning to future troublemakers. He had a decent burial in the churchyard at Kronberg where he had served, although his superior debated whether the body ought to be buried in consecrated ground.

Meanwhile an Augustinian took over mass at Kronberg, since there were no Dominicans about to replace Heidrich. It was a shocking way for a priest to die, even an unscrupulous one like Heidrich. With the new monk giving mass, however, the Kronbergers' attendance at services doubled.

Tilman enjoyed thinking back over the past weeks. For the first time he felt at home on the roughly paved square of Wittenberg, which in his eyes had suddenly changed from a dumpy little pigsty with scarcely two hundred houses to a gentle university town with a rosy future.

In the four months he had lived in Wittenberg, he

had come to love the old town, despite its narrow cobbled streets and its thatched roofs and the chickens running loose in the square. Although he still was not completely at ease in a town where Luther had raised his voice against Mother Church, he did acknowledge the monk's sincerity. Of Luther's methods he could not fully approve.

Swabbing the woodcut with linen rags gave Tilman considerable trouble. The water tended to collect in the smaller cavities—the circles of the o's and a's and e's. He scratched at them with a wooden pick and daubed them with alcohol, but they dried very slowly.

A pounding at the door was followed by the hurrying feet of Eberhard Bostler, who shared the back hall with Tilman. He dashed almost immediately to the master. "Can Tilman come with me, Master Melchior? They've put a notice on the Schwarzes Brett. There's a book burning at the Elstertor."

"A book burning, eh? We spend days printing them and then they burn them. Well, at least it's good for business." He spoke in fun but there was a touch of irony in what he said. As well as anyone, Melchior realized that the church's official attitude toward printing was one of hostility. What could be passed from professor to student or bishop to priest by word of mouth was quite acceptable, but to print books was dangerous, sometimes opening the floodgates of controversy. Therefore the church opposed printing—except, of course, what Rome printed.

"It's on the university bulletin board, Master. It's not Luther's books they're burning. It's the pope's!"

Melchior relaxed. He had seen enough of mobs to know that those who burned books sometimes smashed the shops of printers. "Yes, he can go, for an hour or two. We've spilled water on the press, and we can't print anyway."

Without knowing what he was in for, Tilman threw on his jacket and hurried to the street. The air had a sharp chill, although a warm sun earlier in the week had melted the latest snow. The boys hurried along the Juristengasse and crossed the stone bridge of the Rische Bach.

The square glittered with the first touches of Christmas. The merchants had swung fronds of fir from door to door, and the counters were decked with costly wares that most Wittenbergers could not afford. The fancy cannonballs of cheese or a dangling goose might have been within their pocketbooks, but the fine leather from Tunis, the gold brocade from Damascus, the lace from Bombay, the filigree from the Bosporus, the glassware from Venice, the silk from Acre, not more than forty townsmen could afford even with a prod from their wives. Even Melchior, who was hardly a poor man, thought the finery too costly for his beloved Lotte.

Eberhard chattered excitedly. "It all happened so fast. Today Luther was scheduled to report to Rome. This is the sixtieth day. Or else he was to send a certified letter recanting. Instead, he's made it a holiday."

"Didn't you know about it yesterday?"

"Not a word. At sun-up someone saw Master Melanchthon hurry to the bulletin board. He posted a note inviting students and faculty to gather at nine, for a procession to the burning ground."

"Then you don't know it's a book burning?"

"What else? It's unlawful to build a fire within the walls, for fear of burning the town. The councilmen would raise the roof. Why else go to the burning ground?"

"A speech, maybe?"

"Maybe. But Luther isn't afraid to say anything here he wouldn't say there. No, it must be a burning."

Eberhard's quick, black eyes and spirited chatter created a feeling of expectancy. He thought something important was happening, and he had run all the way to the print shop to get Tilman.

They went through the market and past the bursa. In the street before the monastery a throng of students had gathered.

From the towers of St. Mary's the watchman tolled nine. Out into the Collegiengasse streamed professors and monks, perhaps twenty or thirty, dressed either in the simple frock of the cleric or in the academic capes of the laymen. In their arms they bore bundles of books, with Luther and Melanchthon in the vanguard.

Luther's face was clouded and at the same time jubilant, like a prospective father awaiting his first-born. He talked earnestly with Melanchthon, who was still in his twenties. The close-cropped beard that circled his chin and a thin line of mustache appeared to be a not completely successful effort to make him look mature. Nonetheless, Melanchthon was a man the whole town admired. He was the youngest master at the university and he already had a reputation for knowledge of Greek that attracted students from the farthest corners of Europe—Oslo, Budapest, Lisbon, London, Copenhagen. As a layman he had a certain freedom the monks envied.

Without trying to make a formal procession, the faculty walked two by two out through the Elstertor and across the drawbridge. The students surged behind, at a respectful distance. Atop a pike on the drawbridge the leering face of Turk Stutzer peered down, and on the ash tree beyond the moat his body swung gently from a bough.

Off to the right, in the lowlands of the Elbe, lay an open plot of ground. Usually it served as a slaughtering place or a dumping ground. From an old truss swung the steaming carcass of a sheep, and the two peasants

who flayed it looked up in surprise at the sound of so
many feet.

Luther and Melanchthon were talking earnestly as if
they were out for a Sunday stroll, with little regard for
the other people present. In his black cap, with flaps
pulled down over the ears, Melanchthon could have
passed for a hunter or shepherd. The brim of the cap,
styled like a peaked beret, was broad enough to keep
out rain or snow.

A pile of driftwood had been dragged from the river
bank and piled shoulder high in the middle of the clearing. In a scarlet and blue cape, the university provost
marched forward, said a few words, and touched his
torch to the pile. Almost at once the crackle of flames
echoed among the bystanders.

One after another the faculty stepped to the pyre and
fed the flames with a book. Tilman glanced questioningly at his companion, standing together three or four deep
in the crowd.

"Probably the books Luther has been railing against,
Tilman. Canon law, I would imagine. That's what the
pope uses in his claim to be above Scripture."

A bystander interrupted. "Master Melanchthon gave
the whole list. Canon law, the papal decretals, the Clem-
entines, the writings of Eck and Emser."

On all sides the students whispered excitedly with a

sense of awe at what they were watching. Luther's face showed furrows of concern. He watched the excitement temperately, as if he were only a bystander.

Melanchthon had stepped to the far side of the circle and was talking to ten or twenty of the students. Except for his colorful cape he might have passed for a student, he had such a youthful and exuberant expression. "The pope's agents have been burning Luther's books (not just Luther's—all the evangelical ones) wherever they could get the magistrates' approval. Of course that isn't everywhere. Ingolstadt was the worst." His eyes twinkled with sudden pleasure. "But sometimes the plot backfired. Remember how the University of Louvain jumped into the breach and sided with Eck?"

"Yes."

"Well, when Louvain had their book burning, they couldn't find any of Luther's writings to burn. Only two or three copies in the whole university. So the students pretended to throw in theirs—but they actually threw in Eck's and Emser's and Canon Law." The professor chuckled, as if he had plotted the joke himself, then moved quietly back to Luther's side.

Next to Philip Melanchthon, Luther looked old. He moved nimbly enough, but somehow his face and shoulders gave the impression that he carried the weight of the whole world. Without saying a word he pulled the cincture tight about his waist and stood gazing into the flames.

Obviously the crowd expected a speech. It was for Luther's benefit they had staged the fire, to show their sympathy. Even if the rest of the world anathematized him, they were still proud to stand at his side. As he stood there, lost in his thoughts, it seemed as if he were just an ordinary monk who relished the limelight little.

Tilman saw him pull at his jowl, deep in thought. The flames leaped high and the crowd fell back to escape the heat. Almost by impulse Luther reached inside his cloak and pulled out a vellum scroll. With trembling fingers he read it. More by impulse than forethought he strode to the flames.

He touched one end to a brand and as it caught fire, cast it atop the pyre. His voice was clear and steady. "Since you have twisted the truth of the Lord, may the fires of eternity consume you."

As the bull went up in smoke Luther stepped back to the huddle of faculty. His face bore a look of quiet triumph. For the first time he seemed to be enjoying himself. Melanchthon shook his hand, followed by Schurf and then by all his colleagues. The students stood by in awe, amazed that Luther would burn a papal bull. It was an act of daring they could not have imagined. To burn the works of Eck and Emser was one thing, but to burn the pope's was to shout defiance at the whole church. Tilman looked questioningly at his companion, but he saw no concern in the features of Eberhard.

The faculty dispersed quietly, making their way over the meadows to the drawbridge. In the confusion Tilman was not sure where his sympathies lay. To be honest, he was appalled. Yet he could understand Luther's motives. He thought of the other leaders whom the bull condemned, responsible men like Pirckheimer and Spengler and Carlstadt. Could all these men be wrong too, or had the pope been ill-advised? And when it came to excesses, had not the Papists burned ten times as many books as Luther?

For once in his life Eberhard was so excited his tongue was silenced. His glance darted everywhere, like that of a trial lawyer watching every quirk of the judge and jury.

On the part of the students there was no meditation. In their black capes and caps, unmindful of the chill weather, they were celebrating. Unlike Luther and the professors, who had been solemnly joyful, the students welcomed the ceremony as a much-needed holiday. Little clusters, garbed in outlandish costumes, were scurrying to and fro, carrying pennants on standards.

One of the students had fashioned a golden crown with the three layers of the papal tiara, and he came strutting gleefully toward his buddies with it on his head. With whoops and hollers the crowd ran out to carry him over the meadow. Thrice round the fire they paraded, mock heroes, solemnly knocking the crown from his head, rolling it in the dirt, and finally consigning it to the pyre. As it burst into flames a roar of approval rocked the valley and echoed off the walls.

Eberhard and Tilman edged back from the fire, where they could share its warmth but at the same time hold themselves apart from the celebrators.

In no time three students rattled up in a peasant's cart drawn by a team of oxen. With the sideboards gone, it made a perfect platform for a float. Almost out of nowhere, it seemed, someone had made a giant-size copy of the bull. It was fabricated from three sheets of elephant folio, glued together. The words were so large in the opening paragraph that one could read them ten feet away—*Exsurge, Domine*. "Arise, O Lord, and plead thy cause." The paper was mounted on a crossbar fixed upright in the floor boards. At the tail gate, on a smaller pole, fluttered a sheaf of indulgences, with the bright red seals of Tetzel marking their authenticity. One student waved a sword in the air, over the splashboard, with an indulgence impaled on the blade.

The students drove the cart toward the Elbtor, directly before the square. Dressed in scarlet cloth, six of them climbed aboard and surrounded the bull, like the cardinals who had helped write it. At first the gleeful hubbub was nothing but noise, but as the holidaying became organized, the students broke out into the solemn strains of the funeral mass, chanting the liturgy in Hebrew. Placards picturing Luther's coat of arms, the elector's pennon, the pope's tiara, pierced through with the bolt of a crossbow, sprouted like mushrooms. The wagon creaked across the grasslands and rumbled up onto the planks of the drawbridge. The funeral chant over, the students switched to the *Te Deum.* Atop the parapet the guards smiled benignly. They had seen the faculty out on the meadow and surmised the fun-making was properly approved.

Tilman and Bostler followed at a distance. Neither was quite sure he wanted to be counted a part of the mob. Thinking much but saying little, Tilman walked slowly back to the print shop.

CHAPTER FIFTEEN

THE DAY
OF RECKONING

"You see, Meister Lucas, if I were nineteen or twenty, the answers would be easy. Five months ago, at Torgau, the world looked simple. I thought I knew exactly what I wanted. Now it's all changed."

Cranach was dressed rather elegantly for a painter, in an old silken doublet and a slightly worn pair of velvet breeches, covered with a long smock that bore years of daubs and splashes. He smiled but did not take his hand from the pencil or his eyes from the sheet of folio, sketching the layout of an altarpiece. "I'm flattered, Tilman, that you ask *me*. But the answers are never easy—not about marriage and a career and a place to live. Not about anything, really."

"There's no one I trust as much as you, Herr Cranach.

Miller Zillerthal, of course. But he's a bachelor, and perhaps prejudiced about marriage. And although he seems to have a pleasant income, he doesn't care about his job, just as long as he can bag a grouse and snare a trout and buy a new matchlock."

It was a rather astute characterization for a seventeen-year-old, and Cranach was forced to chuckle. "Herr Zillerthal has suffered many disappointments in life—a mother who did not really love him, and a father who was too fond of the wine keg. You'd be surprised how much he's made of himself, with blessed little help from anyone."

"Sir, it's not that I'm making fun of him. I like him. I've spent a good many hours there. But he knows so little about marriage or business. Compared to you, I mean. He does seem to care about the church, even if I can't completely agree with his views."

The painter looked out over his easel. The sun gleamed from the windows, reflecting from the deep cover of snow in the courtyard. He was laying out a sketch of Christ's Baptism. The vast workshop was active everywhere, with twenty men sketching or painting or sizing canvas or mixing colors or cleaning palettes.

"So you want to marry Ingrid von Tannenlohe, is that it?"

"Yes, sir. I think so. I am so confused I'm not sure. Some day. Some day I want to marry her."

"How old are you, Tilman?"

"Seventeen, sir. Eighteen next Rogationtide."

"And the girl?"

"Fifteen, sir. Sixteen at Whitsuntide."

The painter stood back from his sketch and eyed it at a distance. He smudged one line out and started another. "I can sympathize, boy. Half the youths your age are already married. But you have a fine education and with the gifts you have you can go far. Students, doctors, lawyers, craftsmen—they all get ahead if they postpone marriage."

"Oh, it's not that I want to marry *now*. But if I leave Wittenberg, you see, the chances of coming back are slim. Sometimes I think I could decide better if I were away. About Ingi, and about Luther, and what he's trying to do. Here everyone is so enthusiastic it's hard to be objective. And then there's the printing. I know there's plenty of it in Wittenberg, perhaps as much as anywhere in Germany. But how can a youngster like me get started? I do know something of the trade, and I have a little cash. Forty gulden in a letter of credit at Torgau and the seventeen I got after the robbery. It's not much, I know, but it would buy at least a small press and pay a few months' rent."

"How long have you been thinking this way, Tilman?"

"Almost since I came to Wittenberg, sir." He pointed

"How long have you been thinking this way?"

to a tiny winged figure in the corner. "What's that?"

"That?" Lucas laughed. "That's a bat. A kind of trademark, if you will, to certify that the altarpiece came from the workshops of Lucas Cranach. Even if the work isn't one hundred per cent mine, the faces and outlines are. If the others don't come up with something I approve, we pitch it in the fire. With all the orders I have, it's a crime, but I do have to keep up the quality or I'd be out of business altogether."

The smell of turpentine hung heavy throughout the

studio. With fireplaces on three sides, the room was probably the warmest in Wittenberg. The heat was needed to dry the paint quickly and to keep it at the proper temperature for mixing, even in the dead of winter. It was the week before Christmas, and a foot of snow lay heavy on the roof.

"You've been in Wittenberg four months now?"

"Nearly five, sir. By the spring thaw, it'll be eight."

"Are you learning anything from Melchior?"

"Indeed, yes. He knows more about paper than I dreamed possible. He has a new process for inking the press, too, and a knowledge of the selling trade I couldn't have dreamed of."

"Good. I wouldn't want you to be wasting your time."

"No fear, sir. The others say he's a bit tight with the money, but he's not with me. I *am* learning a lot, the food is unbeatable, and they take good care of the help."

"Fine. Melchior does pinch the pennies. In some ways, that's good, although it's hard on poor Lotte when she wants a new gown."

Hung high on the far wall were six huge canvases. Below, in various stages of completion, was the rest of the series: sketches and canvases, portraits and landscapes.

Cranach followed the eyes of his visitor. "For the bishop's palace at Aschaffenburg. A set on the life and martyrdom of St. Sebastian."

"Isn't that the bishop who fumes against Luther?"

The artist grinned. "So what? He does, as a matter of fact! But it's not a sin to paint the life of a saint. As long as I please God, that's what counts. Of course, I have to please the customers, too, if I'm to keep bread in the mouths of my wife and children."

"You're right—it's just that you're always so outspoken in favor of the Reformation."

A journeyman brought layouts for an *Altarflügel* at Leipzig, discussed shading and color, then strode back to his desk. "Tell me more about Ingrid, Tilman. Do you know her well enough to make a decision?"

"That's what bothers me, sir. When I don't see her, I miss her. In the winter, of course, with the market closed, I don't get to see her often."

"Do you think you love her?"

"Love? I'm not sure I know what it means, except in the songs of the troubadours and minnesingers. I think I could. I'm not really sure."

"You've known the girl only five months. Give it a bit of time, if you're really interested."

"Then you don't think she might marry someone else?"

"Don't fear, lad. Her mother's not the sort to push her on someone she doesn't love. If she herself should choose another, you'd be better off anyway, if it wasn't really *you* she wanted."

"I never thought of it that way."

An apprentice spread out two small parcels on a table beside the master. "The new indigo and umber, Herr Cranach."

The artist sifted a sample in his palm and rubbed it between his fingers. "Good. This will do nicely. Mind you, don't mix more than a cupful at a time. And not too much oil, eh? We can always thin it, if need be, but it's not so easy to thicken again." The apprentice trotted away, with an expression of respect written clearly into his features.

"Have you talked it over with anyone, Tilman—besides Reinhard?"

"No. I guess I haven't, except with Eberhard Bostler, but just about the matter of the printing press and Wittenberg—not about Ingi. He's been interested in the girl too, I think, ever since the day he helped pull her from the Faule Bach."

"Ah, the light begins to dawn. If you leave, Eberhard gets the girl, is that it?"

Tilman glanced at the floor and his face reddened. "Maybe."

"Well, it's true a man has to stay in the race if he wants to win. But don't forget, someone always has to lose. You or Eberhard. And that's the kind of wound, at your age, that will heal a good deal faster than the one from the stag."

"The way I feel about Ingi, I don't even know what to get her for Christmas. I ought to do something, and yet I don't want her to feel obligated. Maybe it ought to be something for the family. Her mother's old copper kettle goes to the tinker's every month to get the seams soldered, and I've just about decided I'll invest twenty groschen in a new one. I've had enough tea out of that kettle to owe them one anyway."

"Will you be spending Christmas there?"

"They've asked me, yes. So has Melchior. And Eberhard's suggested I come to Nürnberg. He even offered to pay the fare."

"You're still undecided?"

"Not really. I'd prefer a few hot chestnuts in the Tannenlohe cottage to goose and mincemeat in Nürnberg."

"Then you're in love."

"I think so."

"Well, that doesn't solve everything, but at least it sheds some light. There's still the Reformation and the printing shop. Even when you're not sure, you sometimes have to stick your neck out."

"So I'm beginning to see."

"Just like on the day of the chase. By instinct you protected those children, without really thinking of the danger to yourself. Well, the Reformation's not so different. Surely by now you've seen enough of Luther to know he's not acting just for himself. Rightly or wrongly, he's convinced something has to be done and he's going ahead with it."

"I wish it were as clear to me as to him—or for that matter, to you. Even the elector seems to have no reservations."

The painter began to blend pigments and to mark the background with the shade he wanted. "The elector acts as a prince. Luther is *his* subject, *his* professor, in *his* university. The pope claims temporal authority. The elector denies this. If you study the elector's letters, you'll discover that his kindliness to Luther is a matter of principle: state's rights versus church rights. He himself would just as soon be neutral; it's his wife who supports Luther."

"I wish I could be sure Luther is right."

"That's something you'll have to live with. I know you must consider the vows to your mother and your training with the Brothers of the Common Life. Maybe you didn't know it, but Luther studied with the same order, at Magdeburg. But mind, you don't have to decide today. Leo and Luther both have the Gospel. As you grow up you must decide how *you* can best hear God's truth as *you* understand it. No one can answer for you."

Tilman's face reflected a quiet serenity. Even the mop of hair over his forehead did not seem quite so unruly.

"And then there's the business of printing. Even if

I do have some money and know enough about the trade, who would ever deal with a seventeen-year-old? Even if I owned a press, how can I hire a journeyman until I'm five or ten years older?"

"It is a bit of a problem, isn't it? You shouldn't have learned your trade so young, Tilman. Not that there still isn't plenty to learn. You're just too far ahead for your age."

"The problem I know. It's the answer I have to find."

Cranach's secretary interrupted him at the easel. "Sir, it's about the fresco for Munich. The bishop has written to ask for a completion date."

"Ah, yes. With all this snow, it's hard to say. Tell him that. Let's see. I'll send Zimmermann and two of the apprentices. Tell him the middle of March. Earlier, if there's a thaw."

"Yes, Master. And would you sign the order for the apothecary, so we can get it off to Augsburg?"

Lucas ran quickly over the items and quantities— nightshade, sulphur, foxglove, saltpeter, henbane, cobalt, oxide, zinc. He scrawled his name, then put down his brush and walked to the window facing the courtyard. Tilman followed. "I'm not really sure I should make my proposal at all unless you want to stay in Wittenberg. I wouldn't want you to blame *me*, after I'm moldy in the grave, for forcing your hand."

"No, sir." Tilman could not imagine what was coming next, but it must have been important, to get the great man away from his brushes. "I'm not taking up too much of your time, sir?"

"Shades of Hades, no! I'm still working." He had to smile when he saw he was not. "You're worth a dozen paintings, son. It's just that what I offer shouldn't force your hand. You can still make up your own mind. Will you remember that?"

"Yes, sir."

"Well, I've been thinking about this for nearly a month. I haven't said a word to Melchior, although it was he who started the gears turning. He wants to expand, Tilman. He came to ask for a loan. A partnership, really. He'd like to buy a second press and to convert the warehouse next door to a print shop. The whole venture would probably cost eighty or ninety gulden, provided we also bought the roman matrices he wants."

Tilman looked out at the snow still sifting gently into the courtyard. Cut off from the winds it drifted like gentle flecks of flour in the mill. The boy looked into the face of his friend, but said nothing.

"As I indicated, I haven't committed myself, but I encouraged him. He knows his trade; he's a hard worker; the money would be relatively safe. Even before you came to see me, I must admit, I've been considering the possibilities. Do you think you know Melchior and me enough to trust us?"

"Completely."

"Then let me give you something to chew on. Melchior is nearly fifty, and in another ten or twenty years he'll be ready to take life easy. Without sons of his own, who knows who'll get the print shop? If I'm going to invest, I'd like some assurance the shop will go on making money."

The painter pulled a rag from his smock and wiped the soot from the leaded panes. "This is what I had in mind. If Melchior is willing to sell half interest, you and I could share it. You know printing, and I know investments. If Melchior should get out of line, our vote would equal his—I don't think he will, of course. He's always been sober and industrious, even if he is a penny-pincher."

The boy's eyes gleamed with interest, and he let the artist continue. "With eighty gulden we could knock down the retaining wall, tighten up the warehouse, buy new matrices, get a second press. There's plenty of room and it's a good solid building. If you should change your mind, I could always buy you out. With the forty gulden from the letter of credit you wouldn't have to touch the seventeen you've got here—save them for buying a house or getting married."

He looked inquiringly to see what effect his words had, then continued. "You and Melchior would also be drawing masters' wages—no, perhaps you'd better stay at the journeyman rates till you're twenty, to keep the guild happy. However, there would be a bonus for keeping the books and supervising—say an extra five gulden a year."

Tilman was so deeply moved he could say nothing. He looked as if he were about to cry. The snow outside no longer seemed cold and unfriendly.

"Mind you, there are plenty of details to work out, but they are not insurmountable. Think it over. If you like, you can give me your answer on Sylvester Eve, after mass. I won't have any trouble persuading Melchior. He needs the money, and he likes you. He's said so. With me in the bargain, it won't be as if he were going into business with his apprentice."

Tilman's voice was low and he could scarcely control it. "Thank you, sir." In the space of a few minutes the problems of his little world seemed to have vanished. "A blessed Christmas, sir." He fumbled at his coat and wrapped a muffler about his throat.

"Give the Tannenlohes my best for Christmas, Tilman. Let me know, will you?"

The boy nodded, but could not find his voice. He did not want to shed an unmanly tear before Lucas Cranach. He left in silence.

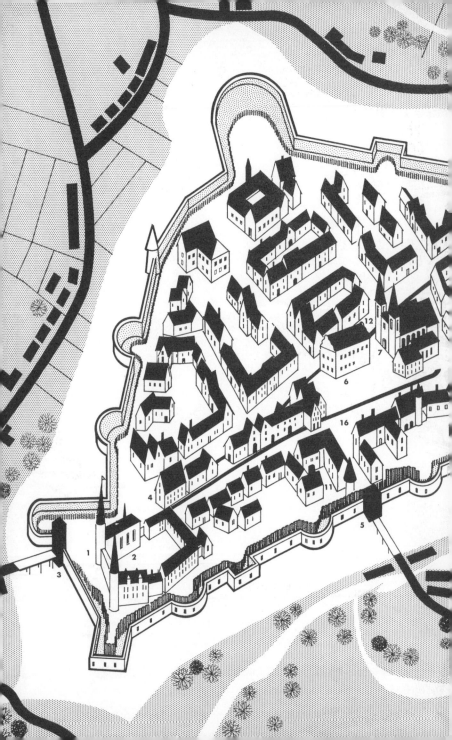